SURPRISE BABY FOR THE HEIR

SURPRISE BABY FOR THE HEIR

ELLIE DARKINS

MILLS & BOON

First published in Great Britain 2019
by Mills & Boon, an imprint of HarperCollins*Publishers*
1 London Bridge Street, London, SE1 9GF

Large Print edition 2019

ISBN: 978-0-263-08247-0

This book is produced from independently certified
FSC™ paper to ensure responsible forest management. For
more information visit www.harpercollins.co.uk/green.

Printed and bound in Great Britain
by CPI Group (UK) Ltd, Croydon, CR0 4YY

For Tess

CHAPTER ONE

'SO, WHO DO YOU HATE? The bride or the groom?'

Elspeth frowned at the sound of the stranger's voice behind her. She turned to look and realised that she'd noticed this guy earlier. How could she not? Even among the sea of tartan and kilts he stood out. He was taller and broader than most of the other men filling the Royal Botanic Garden in Edinburgh, and his red hair had obviously been dragged into some sort of order at the start of the day but had been progressively rebelling ever since.

With her mouth open to tell him to leave, Elspeth realised that the man was already pulling up a chair to sit beside her, man-spreading with a confidence that showed just how comfortable he was in a skirt.

'Neither, of course,' she said, faking a smile,

conscious that she was only at this wedding for appearances' sake, and clearly not doing a good enough job of keeping up the appearance of wedding joy.

'Then why do you look upset?' her new friend asked, looking at her astutely.

'Maybe I just have one of those sad faces.'

She wasn't sure why she'd answered him, given that it wasn't actually any of his business. She'd been wearing her best corporate fake smile for the best part of six hours, through the most ironically torturous day of her life. What was it to this guy if she'd let it slip for three minutes while everyone else had eyes on the bride and groom's first dance.

'Long story,' she added with a sigh.

She wondered briefly why she hadn't just shut the conversation down, as she'd originally intended. Perhaps something about the scene playing out in front of her was making her sappy. Or perhaps it was today's date—the one she'd inked into her diary with a simple 'my wedding'. Or the fact that this was the venue that she'd booked for her own nuptials. And the flowers were the ones that she'd chosen, and the food was the exact menu she'd tasted for the first time a little under a year ago.

In fact, the whole day had been the wedding that she'd spent a year planning and then had been faced with dismantling when she had split with her fiancé with just six months to go before their big day.

She remembered coming into the office the morning after they'd called it all off, eyes red and skin tight from lack of sleep, to find her boss, Janet, proudly showing off a diamond ring. And it had seemed that before she knew what was happening her boss was offering to take over all Elspeth's reservations, saving her from losing the deposits, so that she could have a whirlwind wedding.

She'd turned it into more of a circus than Elspeth had intended, of course, chucking in a hundred extra guests and adding a few zeroes to the budget. But her own wedding had been visible enough to sting throughout the day, like little brushes of nettles against her bare arms everywhere she turned.

She couldn't make herself regret it, though—the cancellation of her wedding or agreeing to the takeover. It made financial sense. Elspeth couldn't afford to lose the money, so she'd gone along with it, happily in denial about the whole thing until the invitation had arrived and she'd realised that she was expected to attend.

If she hadn't needed to impress everyone at the GP practice in order to be offered a permanent role when her training post ended she wouldn't be here. But she needed financial security, and that meant turning up, smiling, and making sure her boss never saw how much she was hating this.

Turned out she'd been doing such a shoddy job that a complete stranger had already rumbled her.

Elspeth took solace in the fact that on her wedding day Janet was hardly going to be paying her much attention. As long as Elspeth appeared in the photos and was mentioned in the inevitable office chat about the event on Monday morning it would hopefully be enough.

But for now she should really get rid of this man. The last thing her misery needed today was company. She just had to get through watching the first dance, and the cutting of *her* cake, and then she could go home.

A stiff drink was the answer.

She stood and headed to the bar, wondering whether he would follow her. The sensible part of her—the part of her she usually left in charge—hoped that he wouldn't. That she could just drown her sorrows in private. But there was something about the mischief in his eyes, something promising trouble, that had her intrigued. That made her want to ignore the part of her brain that had kept her together and her fear at bay for as long as she could remember.

'So, if you don't hate either of them, what's this long story about?'

Elspeth's stomach swooped at the soft sound of his voice behind her, his presence by her shoulder making her skin tingle in awareness. That answered her question, then. She'd been hoping for more of him.

'I'm not sure I want talk about it,' she said, lifting one of the flutes of champagne laid out on trays on the bar and taking a long sip as she turned to him.

He gave her an easy, relaxed smile, grabbing a glass for himself before leaning back against the bar. 'Well, will you at least let me try and distract you from it?'

Any way he wanted.

Wow, when her mind went there, it really went for it, she realised, as a host of ideas for how they could distract one another flooded her consciousness.

She studied him closely over the rim of her glass. 'Why would I do that?'

Just because her body was telling her in no uncertain terms what she wanted, that didn't mean she couldn't have a little fun with this.

He was still leaning against the bar, the picture of casual insouciance. 'How about because I'm also here under duress. I hate weddings—and I don't understand anyone who doesn't. I thought having an accomplice might be fun.'

Elspeth narrowed her eyes as she looked at him. Really, the only thing she wanted was to get out of here. But, as she couldn't do that until the formalities were out of the way, perhaps this would pass the time. And then there was the fact that her eyes kept being drawn to the calves exposed beneath his kilt, and to the way his hair was determinedly escaping whatever order it had been dragged into earlier. And the way those green eyes watched her, promising trouble if she wanted it.

'An accomplice? What exactly are you planning?' she asked. 'I could do without being arrested, so if we can keep it just this side of legal… But go for it. Do your worst.'

'In that case, would you like to dance?'

Elspeth glanced over her shoulder at the dance floor to see that it was filling with guests, joining the bride and groom, who were still wrapped around one another in the centre of the floor.

She laughed. 'That's it? That's your grand plan to distract me from my misery? Dancing in that syrupy mass?'

His eyes flicked to follow her gaze. 'Fair point. What about we cause a diversion, sneak something from the bar and go explore the gardens instead?'

Elspeth glanced around her and realised the bar was unattended and all eyes were still on the bride and groom on the dance floor. With a quick grin at her accomplice, she reached casually across the bar and snagged a bottle of champagne by the neck, then twisted her arm to hide it behind her back.

'Okay, so you really went for it. Good for you. I'm Fraser, by the way. I think we should probably be on first-name terms if we're embarking on a crime spree together.'

She widened her eyes at him in mock innocence. 'I'm sorry, I don't know what you're referring to. But I think I need some fresh air. Care to join me?'

Elspeth felt a shiver as Fraser draped an arm around her shoulder and tried not to think what anyone watching might be thinking. Maybe it was better that they thought they were sneaking out for a quickie or a snog, than realising that she was sneaking away with a very nice bottle of champagne.

He was using his body to shield the bottle from view, she reminded herself as her own body warmed beneath his touch. That was the only reason for him to be standing so close that it was making the hairs on her arms prickle.

Elspeth stepped out onto the decking and

wrapped her arms around herself as the chill of the Scottish evening hit her.

Fraser grabbed a blanket from a pile that had been left in a basket by the door and draped it around her shoulders. She looked up and met his eyes, and only then realised how close they were. The sun was hitting the horizon behind him, making the light on the deck golden and glowing.

At her wedding they'd have been having photos taken now, she remembered. Her ex-fiancé, Alex, was a keen amateur photographer, and had scheduled a number of photography sessions into their day.

She shook off the memory of Alex, and the hurt on his face when she'd finally called time on their engagement. By then he'd known as well as she had that a marriage between them would never work. He'd wanted her to choose. To put him at the top of her priorities, even above her family.

But she was the one who'd actually ended it. Who had said that the compromises he wanted from her weren't going to happen. That she couldn't let anyone else take care of her family. That if he wanted to be with her he would have to accept that he would have to share her.

She took a step back from Fraser, breaking the connection between them and walking out across the deck.

'So, do you want to tell me this long story?' Fraser asked, following behind her.

'I thought you were meant to be cheering me up,' she replied, turning and looking over her shoulder as she reached the railing, leaning on it and looking out over the botanic gardens. 'Trust me, talking about things isn't going to be cheery for either of us.'

'Ah, but we have this to help us,' Fraser said, slipping an arm beneath the thick woollen blanket he'd wrapped around her and taking the bottle.

He ripped the foil from the neck of the bottle and started untwisting the wire cage around the cork.

Elspeth eyed the bottle. 'We'll need more than that.'

Fraser lifted an eyebrow as he twisted the cork, then pressed his thumbs beneath it. 'Sounds ominous.'

'Well, let's just say that today has come with a massive sense of *déjà vu*. Or future *vu*, or something weird like that.'

'You had a vision that you'd be stealing champagne from a free bar with a stranger in a kilt?'

She grinned involuntarily. 'Yes, this is what I planned for my Saturday night. Attending my own wedding as a guest and stealing the booze.'

'*Your* wedding?'

Elspeth let out an ironic laugh, wishing her tongue wasn't so easily loosened by alcohol. God, maybe she should just say it. Burying it and pretending these feelings didn't exist wasn't making the day bearable. Time to try something different.

'I was meant to be getting married today.'

She stated it baldly, with as little emotion as she could manage, but even she could hear the waver in her voice. Fortunately the cork popped out of the bottle with perfect comic timing, and Fraser directed the spilling white foam into her glass.

'Well, I wasn't expecting that,' he said, slightly

flustered, in the classic manner of a man who has just been hit by an emotional confession he hadn't expected. 'Quick—drink,' he added, as the bubbles reached the top of the glass and threatened to spill over.

Elspeth drank, seeing no better course of action, and spluttered slightly at the tickle of the exploding bubbles in her nose. She laughed, fully out loud this time—the first genuine laugh she'd managed all day.

Correlation wasn't causation, and all that, but maybe Fraser was on to something, encouraging her to talk about what was going on. She did feel a little better. A willing ear from a stranger could be as good as therapy—and cheaper.

'I was meant to be getting married here, actually,' she went on. 'I called it off a few months ago and the day after my boss got engaged. She offered to take over my reservations…save me losing my deposits.'

'Wow,' Fraser said, holding the champagne bottle hovering just above his glass, frozen in the second of pouring.

'You said that already,' Elspeth remarked,

raising her brows as she took another sip of wine, enjoying having him on the back foot.

He had been so cocksure, swaggering up to her, asking her to dance, suggesting they get into trouble together. It felt good to turn the tables: see him lost for words.

'And you decided you wanted to come because…what? You're a sadist?'

'I think that would make me a masochist, actually.' She dropped the word casually, as if her sudden thought of kinky sex with this gorgeous stranger had had absolutely zero effect on her heart rate. 'And, no, sorry to disappoint, if that's your thing, but I'm here because the bride is my boss and I was invited.'

He nodded sagely, thankfully not acknowledging her veiled question about his sexual kinks. She wasn't sure it would be good for her to hear exactly what he was into in the bedroom. Her mind was having plenty of fun making up the details by itself.

'Some big promotion in the offing?' Fraser asked, and it took Elspeth a moment to remember what he was talking about.

She took a sip of her drink and nodded. 'Something like that.'

'You're a doctor?' he said, after clearly searching through his memory banks for the bride's profession.

'A GP, yes. Well, a trainee, and hoping for a job when I finish.'

'Why did you want to be a doctor?'

Elspeth couldn't remember the last time someone had asked her that. And she didn't have a good answer. To her, it had never seemed like a choice. All she knew was that it had been a decision made long before she had chosen her exam subjects as a teenager. Probably around the time she had been sitting by her baby sister's bedside, incapable of doing anything that could help her other than sit there.

She'd trained as a doctor because she wanted to help people like Sarah. Be their advocate in the healthcare system and ensure that every single one of them got the best outcome that they could. Because she had seen the miracles the medical profession could perform. Keeping her sister alive, getting her home, giving her independence with an electric wheelchair and communication aids, among the million other ways it had helped her over the years.

And now Elspeth had the skills and the knowledge she hadn't had when Sarah was a baby, which meant she could be cared for by her family rather than by strangers. But her care responsibilities meant careful planning for the future, especially given that her mum had been in her forties when Sarah had been born, had arthritis herself, and wasn't going to be mobile, or even around, for ever.

But that was way more detail than anyone needed to know—especially dangerous-looking men in kilts brandishing bottles of champagne.

'I liked science and I wanted to help people,' Elspeth said, giving the standard medical school application answer.

It wasn't really much of an explanation, but it was all he would be getting. She had watched her relationship with Alex dissolve around her because he hadn't been able to reconcile family and romance, but she had no desire to go into the details. Perhaps talking about this wasn't the good idea she'd thought it might be.

'Anyway,' she said, keen to change the topic of conversation and shift the attention away from her sorry tale. 'That's my story. What's yours? Why are *you* here if it's so tortuous?'

Fraser shrugged as he leant his forearms against the railing, surveying the gardens in front of them. 'Nothing so exciting—just family duty. The groom is my mum's cousin. My mother insisted I be dragged into groomsman duty to make up the numbers even though I hardly know the guy.'

'Ah, a mummy's boy,' Elspeth said with a smile, echoing Fraser's knowing tone from earlier. 'Interesting…'

Fraser bumped her shoulder with his and Elspeth held her hands up.

'Hey, if it sounds like a duck, looks like a duck, and does what Mama Duck says…'

'Enough—drink your wine,' he said with a laugh, topping up her glass again. 'I did *not* lure you out here to talk about my mother.'

'Now, *that* sounds interesting.'

Elspeth looked up at him, pulling the blanket a little tighter around her shoulders, hyper-aware of the scratch of the fabric on her shoulders, the earthy smell of the wool, the barrier it put between her and Fraser.

'I'm not sure I remember being *lured*, as such. But what were your motivations if you weren't thinking about introducing me to your mother?'

Oh, she was sure that asking that question was going to get her into trouble. But that twinkle in his eye, the way he challenged her with his stare, egging her on, had tweaked at something inside her. She wanted to play.

He smiled back at that slight suggestion of innuendo, and she knew that she was right. She'd just got herself into trouble and she couldn't bring herself to be sorry about it.

'So you're saying you're not the kind of girl I want to take home to meet the parents, huh? Well, that's good to know. I thought we were going to explore out here. Wasn't that the plan?'

Elspeth drained her glass and gestured towards the steps down from the decking. 'Lead on. Where do you want to look first?'

They wandered through the gardens, their shadows long over the lawns, until they came across a gathering of redwood trees: Californian giants, hundreds of feet tall. Beneath their shade, the light was lost completely, and Elspeth realised what a secluded spot they had found.

She leant back against the trunk of one of the trees, feeling small, humbled by the scale of them. As Fraser approached, still swinging the bottle by his side, Elspeth held up her glass like a shield, suddenly aware of the intimacy of their surroundings, how her attraction to Fraser had been bubbling under the surface of their banter since he had first approached her, and how he was looking at her now, like the wolf in a fairy tale.

But she was no innocent Red Riding Hood, and she had no plans to run or hide.

'Do you think we've missed them cutting the cake?' Elspeth asked, breaking the tension, wondering whether they'd come too far to take their conversation back to something inane and safe.

'I'm not sure.' Fraser came closer, topping up her glass, then closer still, so she wouldn't have been able to lift it to her lips if she'd wanted to.

The glass was trapped against her chest, along with her hands and her resolve. 'Do you care?'

'Not really.' The words escaped her before she could stop them, but she couldn't regret them. Not when they lit a spark in Fraser's eyes that made the night seem a little less dark.

'You don't want to go back?'

Oh, there was so much more to that question, and she could see from the look in his eyes, lit only by the moon, that he knew it.

Surely it was late enough by now that she wouldn't be missed at the reception? In her plan for the day, that was meant to be her cue to leave. To get home to her mum and her sister. Not to slope off somewhere with a stranger she would probably never see again.

Because if there was one thing she was sure about when it came to this connection she felt to Fraser, it was that it was never going to last more than a night. She had tried balancing a relationship, her work and family commitments before, and it hadn't been possible. She'd got hurt. Alex had got hurt. And she knew her family had been hurt too, as they'd seen all their hopes for her unpicked and falling away.

But one night with this man—well, that could be something interesting. More and more, it was feeling as if it could be something irresistible.

'I don't want to go back,' she said, looking up to meet his eyes, making sure that he couldn't mistake her meaning.

She let the tree take her weight, surrendering herself to her decision, to her desire. The champagne glass slipped from her hand and she heard it hit the ground with a soft rustle. With her hands free, she brushed the front of Fraser's jacket, taking a moment to really feel the fabric, the softness of well-worn wool on her fingertips. From his lapels she stroked upwards, inwards, and heavy fabric gave way to soft cotton.

His eyes never left hers as she reached the studs of his shirt and hooked her fingers into the fabric, pulling him down to her.

'What do you want?' Fraser asked, breaking their look at last and glancing down at her hands.

'I think you know.'

'Oh, I've got a pretty good idea. But I want to hear you say it.'

'It's going to be like that, is it?' Elspeth asked with a shiver, hoping very much that it would be.

He was still looking at her as if he wanted to consume her, and she was good with that. She had too much in her head. Too much in her life. She wanted to be devoured, to devour. To lose herself in her senses, in the present. To be so overwhelmed that she couldn't think about anything beyond the next second.

She slipped her foot out of her shoe and hooked it around Fraser's calf, noticing the feel of every hair that slipped beneath the arch of her foot, the line of his calf muscle, taut and defined and bared to the elements.

As she slipped her foot higher, feeling the slide of his skin beneath hers, she couldn't help imagining what she would find higher still. Wondering whether he was exposed to the elements, to her, beneath that kilt.

With the fingers of one hand still hooked in his shirt, keeping him close, she lifted the other to the back of his neck, feeling the softness of the hair curling at his collar. Meeting his eyes again, she smiled.

'Enjoying yourself?' Fraser asked, with a smile just the right side of smug.

'You know I am,' she murmured, dropping her eyes to his mouth and finding herself unable to look away from it.

She licked her lips, and watched as his mouth curved into a knowing, confident smile.

'Good. Don't stop.'

She had absolutely no intention of stopping. Gripping the front of his shirt tighter, she twisted the fabric between her fingers as she pulled him down to her. She held her breath as she closed her eyes, stretching up on tiptoes until at last her lips brushed against his. Sensation exploded at the touch of his warm mouth and she let out a quiet moan, revelling in every physical sensation assaulting her body.

In the press of hard wood and soft woollen blanket behind her, the creased cotton and tweed in front. The curling hair and soft skin beneath her hand. And the uninhibited mouth on hers. Tasting her, tempting her. Teasing her with its tongue and its lips.

Fraser's arms wrapped around her waist, pulling her away from the tree into his solid chest. Elspeth let her lips trace the line of his jaw until she was close enough to whisper in his ear.

'Let's go.'

Fraser woke to the sensation of silk sheets beneath his body and a warm summer breeze caressing his back. And soft, soft lips pressing against his.

Elspeth.

With his eyes still closed, he wound fingers into her hair, cupped his other hand around her cheek and kissed her lazily, slowly remembering the night before. He pulled her down on top of him, but she stiffened, drawing away until his body and his bed felt cold.

'Bye, Fraser.'

He lifted his head and blinked his eyes at the sound of high heels on deep carpet, heading towards the door, and it was only in the dawn light creeping round the edge of the curtains that he saw Elspeth's face.

'Bye.'

He croaked out the word and then fell back on the pillow as the door closed behind her.

He didn't have her number.

The thought occurred to him and then he was sitting up without realising he'd decided to, and he had a foot out of the bed before he'd thought about what he was doing. Before he stopped himself, as he always had before.

No strings. They'd never actually said the words last night, but it had been clear enough in the way they had been with each other. Well, if he'd had any doubt she'd just proved it by walking out with barely a kiss goodbye.

For a fraction of a second he wondered if he could catch her before the lift reached their floor, but that summer breeze brushed him again, colder this time, and he realised what he was thinking.

He didn't do relationships. He'd seen when he had still been barely more than a child the harm they could do. What happened to people and their lives when they followed their desires rather than making sensible, objective decisions.

He'd sworn that he wouldn't make the same

mistakes. Just the fact that he was even thinking of acting on a whim now was all the proof he needed that it would be a bad idea. Of all the women he might have a second date with, the one who was making him question all his carefully set ground rules was not the one to try it with.

He collapsed back, letting his arm fall over his eyes as he remembered falling into this same bed last night, with Elspeth pulling at his clothes and her body warm and supple beneath him.

Last night wasn't going to be easy to forget. *She* wasn't going to be easy to forget.

CHAPTER TWO

ELSPETH THREW DOWN her work bag by the door and shouted out as she walked through the hallway. 'Mum? Sarah?'

'In here,' her sister called back from the direction of the kitchen.

Elspeth crossed the hallway and smiled at the sight of the pair of them at the kitchen table, the huge pan of chicken and pasta she'd left in the fridge the day before sitting between them. Thank God. She was starving. All she wanted to do was carb-load and fall straight into bed. Again. She'd not made it past nine o'clock a single night this week, and she wasn't planning on breaking her streak tonight.

Her patients had been back to back from eight o'clock that morning, and the only food she'd had all day was a sandwich at her desk while she caught up on notes and phone calls.

She was used to the workload, to the stress and the non-stop appointments, but for some reason this week it had caught up with her. Her body felt heavy, weary in a way she'd not felt since she'd been caught in an endless cycle of night shifts, studying and revision in her first years as a junior doctor.

She just had one last thing to do before she went to help Sarah with her evening routine of medication, personal hygiene and changing for bed.

She had to pee on a stick.

It was just a formality, really. Just to rule out the flashing light that her inner doctor wouldn't allow her to ignore. She was a week or so late, but that wasn't unusual. She'd never had a cycle she could set the clock by. And she'd never taken risks—she always used a condom. But if she'd had a patient sitting in front of her, complaining of the sort of fatigue she had been feeling, she would have ordered a pregnancy test, so it only made sense to rule it out.

She smiled through dinner with her mother and Sarah, listening to stories of their day. Her mother's at work, her sister's at college. But in the back of her mind she couldn't shake off the thought of that little test sitting at the bottom of her bag.

As soon as her fork hit an empty plate she tidied the kitchen, thanked her mum for dinner, made her excuses and headed upstairs. Locking the bathroom door behind her, she thought for the thousandth time what a luxury it would be to be able to leave the door unlocked, free from the fear that her mum or Sarah could walk in on her.

Living at home in her thirties wasn't exactly ideal. But with her mum in her sixties, it wasn't fair to expect her to take on the full responsibility of caring for her sister. They all worked hard to ensure that Sarah was living as independently as possible, but she still required extra support and Elspeth was determined that her mother wouldn't have to take on all that herself. And she wanted to be able to buy a house. Somewhere for her and Sarah to live—a home that they could be certain would always be theirs—and that meant staying at home and saving for a deposit.

Elspeth peed on the test and set it on the

side of the bath as she glanced at her watch. Three minutes and she'd be able to dispel this nagging doubt and get her head on the pillow. Which meant she had three minutes during which she could legitimately let herself think about Fraser.

Because for the past three weeks she'd not let herself do that. She'd pushed her memories of that incredible night out of her mind, knowing that with all the responsibilities in her life she couldn't afford the luxury of a relationship. No matter how good the sex had been. And, *oh*, it had been good. Better than good. Better than sex, actually. Because for those few hours there had been a connection between them. They had laughed, joked, challenged each other.

And when the sun had crept over the horizon in the morning she had crept out of his bed with a sigh of regret, wishing for a moment that her life could be different.

But here, in the cold, stark light of the bathroom, she knew that it couldn't be. She had responsibilities, and she and Alex had already done a fine job of proving that those responsibilities were not compatible with a romantic relationship.

It was a sobering thought, she realised as she kept her eyes averted from the pregnancy test. Looking ahead to a life without romance. Without marriage. Without a family of her own.

Elspeth loved her mum and her sister. She was devoted to them, and it was no sacrifice to set aside what she might want for herself for what was best for her family. But that didn't mean she wasn't curious. That she didn't wonder what sort of life she might have had if her decisions had been her own to make. Maybe she would have been peeing on one of these sticks hoping for it to show a smiley pregnant face rather than dreading the result.

She glanced at her watch. Three minutes. Well, there was no point putting it off any longer. All she had to do was check the test, put her daydreams and her sister to bed, and then climb in between the sheets herself.

She turned the test over.

Pregnant.

For a second she wished she'd bought one of

those cheap, old-fashioned tests. Where you had to scrutinise the stick and the leaflet to work out if there was a line. What the line meant.

Seeing the truth just sitting there, so unvarnished, was a blow to her chest. She couldn't pull in air and sat heavily on the side of the bath, staring at it, unable to tear her eyes away.

She was pregnant. She did the maths in her head. Just a few weeks. Six weeks gestational age, at most. Barely a grouping of cells.

She had options. She ran through them as she would for any patient who wanted them, and in her head she was halfway through the referral process to end her pregnancy before she realised that the thought of doing so made her feel sick. Sick in her stomach, sick in her bones.

She realised that it wasn't the right choice for her.

And that was it, Elspeth thought, as she looked at herself in the mirror. Decision made. She was having a baby.

As she walked out of the bathroom Elspeth could hear her sister typing in her bedroom, and she knocked on the door before pushing it open.

'Hey, sis. Ready for bed?'

Sarah smiled and turned her head, gesturing for Elspeth to sit. 'What's up, Els?' she asked, frowning. 'You're completely white. You're not going to throw up, are you? If you are, you can get off my bed.'

Elspeth pulled a face, feigning ignorance. 'I'm fine. How was college today?'

Sarah gave her an insightful look. 'We already talked about that. Don't change the subject. You look terrible.'

'Gee, with a sister like you…'

'I know—who needs friends? But I'm not letting you off that easy. Come on. Tell me what's up.'

Elspeth considered her options. It wasn't as if she could keep it a secret for ever. And she could do with talking about what was on her mind. Maybe if she said the words out loud they would start to feel more real.

'I—' Her voice broke, stuck behind a lump in her throat. She coughed, took a deep breath and tried again. 'I'm pregnant.'

She heard the words for the first time, but it still didn't help. It felt as if she was talking about someone else. Except for the look on Sarah's face. That made it a little more real.

'Okay. Whose is it?' she asked after a long pause. 'Not Alex's?' she added, looking aghast.

'No,' Elspeth said, unable to help smiling at her sister's horror at the prospect that she was back with her ex. 'It's someone…new,' she said eventually, not sure she wanted her sister to know she'd been picking up strange men at weddings. 'We're not really in touch at the moment.'

They weren't meant to be in touch at all. Not if it meant trying to cram a relationship into a life that she'd already proved had no space for one.

'Guess that's going to have to change,' Sarah said.

Elspeth threw her a look only an older sister could give. 'You're very insightful tonight,' she said.

Sarah turned her chair so that she was looking directly at Elspeth. 'You're the one throwing bombshells. I'm just trying to keep up. How long have you known?'

'I've just found out,' Elspeth said. 'Don't tell Mum. Not till I've had a chance to speak to her first.'

'Of course,' Sarah said, watching her more closely than Elspeth was comfortable with.

Elspeth picked up a book from Sarah's bed, fiddling with it in her hands, running scenarios through her head, none of which were helping.

'Can you grab my pyjamas?' Sarah asked, with a glance at her restless fingers. 'I'm not getting anywhere with this essay. I think I need to sleep on it.'

'Of course,' Elspeth replied, pleased to have the distraction. As she went through the nightly routine—helping Sarah in the bathroom, dressing her, administering her meds and going through her physio regime—her thoughts kept drifting back to Fraser, as hard as she tried to keep them in the present moment.

'Are you going to tell me about him?' Sarah asked, and Elspeth realised she had been looking out of the window for the past few minutes,

Sarah's toothbrush in her hand, completely forgotten about.

'I'm not sure there's much to tell. I haven't known him long. I don't even know if he's going to want to be involved. I mean, *we've* done okay, haven't we?'

Sarah gave her a look that wasn't at all difficult to interpret.

'I know, I know… I'll tell him. I know that I have to. It's just… Don't be surprised if he doesn't stick around, you know?'

Sarah rolled her eyes. 'Don't judge them all by Alex's standards.'

'He wasn't—' Elspeth started to defend her ex. It hadn't been his fault that she hadn't been able to commit to their relationship. She had been asking too much from him—way too much—and she hadn't been surprised when he had taken the escape route she had offered him.

But Sarah interrupted her before she could explain. 'Save it, Els. You know he wasn't the one for you. I've got higher hopes for this new one.'

'You don't know a thing about him.'

'Exactly. I don't know a thing about him other than the look he's put on your face and I already like him more than the last guy.'

CHAPTER THREE

FRASER STARED INTO his coffee and could tell without having to glance at the mirror opposite him that his eyebrows were pulling together in a way that was giving him a line between them.

He was pretty certain that this was a bad idea.

His usual practice when he had unexpected text messages from one-night stands he'd thought he'd never hear from again was to say a polite but firm no, and he should have stuck to that today.

It wasn't that he didn't like spending time with women—he liked to have fun. But he'd seen first-hand what happened when you let yourself be swept away by emotions. Lust and passion were all well and good for a night or two. But when you gave in to them for longer than that they clouded your judgement and led to the people around you getting hurt.

He got hurt.

That was what he had learned as a teenager, when he'd seen his father throw away twenty years of marriage and move in a woman who hadn't lasted more than a couple of years. But when Fraser had given him an ultimatum—'*Either she goes or I do!*'—in the early, heady days of that relationship, his father had chosen his new partner instead of his son.

So Fraser had packed up his things, helped his mother into the car—with her white face and her shocked silence—and left his home, the ancient seat of his ancestors and his title. The estate he had been preparing to inherit from the day he was born.

And he didn't know if he would ever get them back. All because his dad hadn't been able to say no to a pretty face and walk away. Seeing what that had done to his mother had made the decision for him. Nothing and no one, no relationship, could be worth the sort of pain that she had gone through.

Meeting with Elspeth now went against

every rule he had made for himself and stuck to so rigidly for the past fifteen years. But she had found his phone number somehow and invited him for coffee.

She was clearly keen. Keener than most. And that meant he had to be even firmer than usual. He had to tell her, face to face and in no uncertain terms, that he wasn't interested. He didn't do relationships. He'd assumed that she'd known that when she'd taken him home halfway through a wedding and then barely woken him for a goodbye kiss the following morning. Had assumed that she wasn't after anything serious.

So why had she tracked him down? The time for swapping numbers had come and gone without either of them suggesting it, and he had assumed that meant that she felt the same way he did.

Whatever. The whys of the situation didn't matter. All that mattered was shutting this thing down. And it seemed more effective to do that in person than by text. He could show her that he really meant it.

And show himself.

Because he'd been thinking about Elspeth far more than was reasonable or desirable over the past few weeks. Perhaps it was the way that she had sneaked out in the half-light of dawn. The colours in the room faded in the early morning, the silhouette of her face the only clear thing.

But that was no excuse. He'd shared plenty of dawn kisses goodbye before and hadn't had any problems forgetting them.

The door of the hotel lounge where he'd suggested they meet opened and he glanced up. Even though he was expecting her, he still felt his stomach dip at the sight of her.

He'd forgotten how petite she was. Her shoulders were half the width of his, and her head barely reached his collarbone. Her ankles and wrists were so tiny he could wrap them with his thumb and little finger. And so sensitive that she'd moaned every time he'd done so. And those freckles over her nose and her cheekbones…like a constellation of stars. He'd stared at them so intensely that night he had been able to see them even when he'd closed his eyes—like the negative image left by a bright light.

And wrapped up in that delicate exterior was a desire and a strength and a passion that had given his six feet and two hundred pounds a run for their money for a whole, blissful night.

But he wasn't meant to be thinking about that, he reminded himself as he schooled his face back into something neutral. He had to remember that this meeting was about breaking things off, not about picking up where she'd left him, naked in bed, wanting more.

'Hi,' Elspeth said as she approached his table.

Her smile was wary and it made his forehead crease again. She was the one who had asked to meet him, so why was she looking so guarded? So very much as if she didn't think being here was a good idea any more than he did?

He stood to kiss her on the cheek—a polite habit, he told himself, rather than anything meaningful. The hand that he dropped to her shoulder met firm, tense muscle, and he realised that she was really nervous.

'Have a seat,' he said. 'What do you want to drink?'

'I'll have tea. Thanks.'

He could see her looking around the richly decorated interior of the hotel lounge as he summoned the waiter with a glance and wondered whether he'd made a mistake, choosing somewhere so intimate. But he hadn't wanted to have this conversation in a crowded restaurant or bustling coffee bar. Though that would have had its advantages… He'd have loved a reason to step away from her right now and catch his breath.

The sight of her had brought memories flooding back, and he wanted some space to remind himself that it didn't matter that she was beautiful. It didn't matter that she was funny. It didn't even matter that they had killer chemistry together. What mattered was that he couldn't trust himself around her, and he had to make sure that she knew this wasn't going to go anywhere.

He ordered her tea, and a fresh drink for himself. Something to do with his hands. To keep them distracted. To try and forget the memory of the delicate bones of her wrists trapped between his fingers.

'Thanks for meeting me,' Elspeth said eventually, gazing at a point somewhere past his left shoulder.

Alarm bells started ringing. There was definitely more to this meeting than he understood, and he didn't like it.

'What's going on, Elspeth?' he asked, his voice brusquer than he had intended. But he couldn't regret it. He had to know what she wanted from him because his body was growing increasingly tense, and the suspicion that this conversation was going somewhere he wasn't going to like was becoming impossible to ignore.

Elspeth took a deep breath, and—finally—looked him straight in the eye. Her face was set defiantly, as if she were expecting a fight, and a shiver travelled the length of Fraser's spine. A flash-forward—a presentiment, perhaps. An acknowledgement that, whatever it was that had put that expression on her face, he wasn't going to like it.

'I'm pregnant.'

The words hit Fraser like a bus, rendering him mute and paralysed. He sat in silence for long, still moments, letting the words reverberate through his ears, his brain. The full meaning of them fell upon him slowly, gradually. Like being crushed to death under a pile of small rocks. Each one was so insignificant that you didn't feel the difference, but collectively they stole his breath and would break his body.

'Are you sure?' he asked.

He didn't know why. She wouldn't be here if she wasn't sure. The look on her face *told* him that she was sure. And he wasn't going to insult her by asking if he was the father—she wouldn't be here if he wasn't.

'I'm sorry. Of course you're sure.'

But this couldn't be happening. He didn't *want* this. He'd seen the danger of giving in to romantic feelings. His mother had married the man she loved and then found herself turfed out and having to start her life again more than a decade and a half later. His father had given in to those feelings a second time, destroyed his family in the process—and with what to show for it? Two ex-wives and a son who hated him.

Fraser had decided a long time ago that that sort of commitment—the family and marriage sort—wasn't something he was interested in. It couldn't possibly be worth the heartache for everyone involved. Okay, so when he looked ahead maybe he *did* see a couple of kids in his life, in between the dogs and the lambs and the horses. But that didn't mean they were a realistic part of the picture, because they didn't come on their own. The thought of committing to any woman was completely off the cards. And to *this* woman—someone who had already caused him too many sleepless nights—it was impossible.

The commitment of raising a child was an unimaginable complication—how could it not be? He was happy with his life the way it was. With a string of casual attachments and the distant thought that one day, when his father was dead, he would return to his family estate and finally do the job he had spent his whole life waiting and working for. Put into practice all the preparations he had been making in the meantime, developing property and managing estates all over Scotland and being responsible for the lives of the people who lived and worked on them.

His father had always impressed upon him as a child that his money and his title came with responsibilities, and he was determined to be worthy of that privilege. In the years since he had left Ballanross he had been training to take up that position. Learning how to make land profitable; investing the small trust he had inherited from his grandfather and turning it into a fortune. Watching this fall and rise of the property market and ensuring that he was on the right side of it, amassing the cash and the property that had gone some way to filling the hole in his life that the loss of the estate had left.

He'd not been able to return home for fifteen years. His father had made it clear that he wasn't welcome in his home or in his life. Even after his dad's second marriage had broken down, when it had turned out that leaving his wife and the mother of his child *wasn't* the cure for a midlife crisis that he had expected it to be, Fraser had not gone back. How could he when his father had made it perfectly clear that he didn't want him in his life?

So he had taken the heartbreaking decision to wait until the land was his before he returned.

But if he had a child… That would change everything. Because that child had every right to know its inheritance. Its place in the world. On their land. How could he deny him or her that?

'Are you going to say anything?' Elspeth asked, breaking into his thoughts at last.

He met her gaze and saw that it had hardened even furthcr—he hadn't thought that was possible. But he could understand why. He'd barely said a word since she'd dropped her bombshell. He needed time to take this in. Surely she could understand that.

'I'm sorry. I'm in shock,' he said. Following that up with the first thing that had popped into his head. 'We were careful…'

'Not careful enough, it seems.'

Her voice was like ice, cutting into him, and he knew that it had been the wrong thing to say. He wasn't telling her anything she didn't know.

Fraser shook his head. He'd never expected

to be so unlucky. Nor had Elspeth, from the look on her face.

'What do you want to do?' he asked, his voice tentative, aware that they had options. Equally aware that discussing them could be a minefield if they weren't on the same page.

'I want to have the baby,' Elspeth said, using the same firmness and lack of equivocation with which she had told him she was pregnant. How someone so slight could sound so immovably solid was beyond him—and it was a huge part of her appeal, he realised. Something he should be wary of, then.

He nodded, though, his chest a little lighter, and realised that he was relieved that was what she wanted. Selfishly glad that she had spared him having to come to a conclusion himself. That picture of his future with children—it was what he wanted, he realised. He couldn't imagine growing old on his land with no one to pass it on to. It wasn't the child that wasn't wanted—it was the relationship, and the woman, and the commitment, and everything that came with it that was completely terrifying him.

'How are you?' he asked.

Elspeth shrugged. 'Tired, hungry. Everything that you'd expect, really. I'm only about eight weeks along. It's still early days, but I called in a favour and got a scan. Everything looks good so far. We've no reason to think that anything will go wrong.'

'That's good,' Fraser said.

His lips involuntarily turned up into a smile. He wasn't even sure why. He couldn't even think about what he was meant to be feeling at this news.

'So, what do we do now?'

What did they do now?

How on earth was *she* meant to know? She'd only been able to see as far as this. As far as telling the father of her child that the child existed. From here on in it was up to both of them to figure it out.

It would help if she had a clue where to start.

She didn't even know the basics about Fraser. Where he lived. Where he was from. His surname…

They'd come back to this very hotel the night

of the wedding, so she didn't have many clues there, apart from the fact that it was one of the most discreetly expensive hotels in the city. She'd gone along with it, surprised, when he'd suggested meeting here.

If she was honest with herself, she was more surprised that he'd agreed to meet her at all. He had money, she gathered, wondering what he would make of her usual coffee shop and feeling suddenly uncomfortable.

'I guess we try and figure out the practicalities,' she said. 'If you want to be involved.'

She'd decided that this was the best tactic. She didn't want to force him to be in their lives if he didn't want to be. This child had every right to know its father, but it also deserved a father who *wanted* to be there. Not someone who was only doing it because they thought that they should.

A harsh look crossed Fraser's face, and Elspeth realised that somehow she'd touched a nerve.

'Of *course* I want to be involved. What kind of person do you think I am?'

She raised her palms. 'I don't know what

kind of person you are, Fraser. All I know so far is that you get bored at weddings and what you like to do in bed. How am I meant to know what you think about kids? So far, this conversation isn't filling me with confidence.'

'I'm sorry,' he said. 'It's a shock.'

'I know that.' She replaced her cup rather too emphatically on the table and reached for a napkin as the liquid sloshed over the side. 'It wasn't exactly easy for me to find this out either. I had plans, you know. I *have* plans. I have responsibilities that don't exactly fit well with an unplanned pregnancy.'

'Of course—your permanent role at work. Have you had any news? I guess a baby's going to throw all your plans out of whack.'

She wasn't sure whether to be impressed that he'd remembered or annoyed that he was making light of the massive upheaval her career was going to have to go through. She decided quickly on the latter. 'Don't you dare be flippant. I need this job, and my career plans are important. I have responsibilities. Responsibilities and a career that are going to be hard enough to make work without you cracking jokes about it.'

Saying the words out loud was making the reality sink in. How on earth was she going to cope? She'd spent the last God knew how many years asking herself that same question. How was she going to care for her sister when her mum was gone? Or when her mum was older and needed a lot of care too? And now a baby in the mix? It was just too much.

She took a long drink of her tea, letting it wash away the lump that was threatening to form in her throat.

'So—what? You want *me* to take the baby?' Fraser asked.

'What? *No*. Are you deliberately making this harder?'

How could he jump to that conclusion? It made her realise that he really didn't know the first thing about her. Any of her friends, her colleagues, anyone who had met her for more than a random night at a wedding would know that she would *never* let someone else raise her child. And here she was, planning on co-parenting with a man who didn't even understand the basics about her.

'What I want, Fraser,' she said, slowly and deliberately, knowing that her temper wasn't going to help this situation, 'is some sort of plan for co-parenting this child that doesn't completely derail everything I need to happen in my life.'

'Well, it might be a bit late for that. Babies have a habit of derailing things.'

It was Fraser's turn to shrug, and she narrowly avoided the temptation of throwing her tea at him. How could he be so damn casual about it? Simply brush away her concerns?

'Well, in this case it can't.' She ground out the monosyllables, her temper still on the up.

At some point she was going to have to tell him about her life. Her responsibilities. The reason she had called off her engagement. And what would she see in his eyes? Pity? Fear? Horror at what he had got himself involved in?

'Okay, are you going to tell me what this is about or do I have to read between the lines and guess? Are you going to throw me a clue?'

Well, it looked as if she was about to find out.

'It's not a secret,' she said. 'I already have caring responsibilities. I have a sister with a disability and a mother who's getting older, whose arthritis is getting worse by the day. I need to get ahead with my career now, because the time will come pretty soon when I'll need the money I've banked, and I'll need to have reached a point in my career when I can work flexibly.'

'You were engaged before?' Fraser said thoughtfully.

Elspeth bristled. 'I'm not sure what that has to do with anything. I'm talking about the baby, here. I'm not proposing.'

'I'm just saying you must have thought at one time that you could have both. I don't want to marry you, Elspeth. I just want to understand you.'

She tried to throw off the feeling that he was criticising her and answered as calmly as she could. 'You're right. At one time I thought that things could be different, and then I proved myself wrong. When my family and my relationship were both suffering because I was being pulled in opposite directions I had to choose, and I chose my family.'

Fraser's face creased, and Elspeth had a moment to see pain in his eyes before he wiped his expression clear.

'What?' she asked, when Fraser's silence stretched.

'Nothing,' he replied.

But she could tell that something she'd said had touched him. Had resonated with him. She knew he was keeping things from her. But why shouldn't he? He barely knew her. Other than the cells dividing and multiplying inside her, they shared nothing in their lives. They might as well be strangers.

Not quite strangers.

Not when she knew the curve of his buttocks and the scratch of his stubble. The deep, bass notes of his groans and the gentle huff of his breath while he slept.

But not familiar either. Unfamiliar enough for her skin to tingle when it sensed him close. New enough for her heart to pick up its pace a little every time her eyes flickered to his face. Enough of an unknown that she had to resist the temptation to reach out and touch his mouth, just to remind herself of how it had felt pressed hard and hot against hers among the giant trees of the botanic gardens.

Elspeth finished her tea and replaced her cup and saucer on the table, wondering where they were meant to take this next.

'So, what do we do now?' Fraser asked.

Elspeth wondered why she was meant to have all the answers. Just because she was the one doing the gestating? But the answer suddenly seemed straightforward enough—not that that made it easy.

'Well, if we both want to be involved in this baby's life, then I guess we ought to get to know one another,' she said.

Then Elspeth's phone buzzed; she glanced at it and gave a start.

'I'm sorry,' she said. 'I have to get back to the surgery. I'll call you soon and we can arrange something. We've got lots still to talk about.'

Fraser stood as Elspeth did, and for an awkward moment he didn't know whether to offer his hand or lean in to kiss her cheek. A look of alarm on Elspeth's face betrayed that she was as confused as he was and she took a step backwards, making either action impossible.

'We'll speak soon, then,' Fraser said. 'Look after yourself,' he added.

And look after our baby.

He didn't say it out loud, but she must have known that he was thinking it. He was still trying to get his head around the fact that he was going to be a father. What would his mother say? She'd be excited—he had no doubt about that. But he was pretty sure that this wasn't how she'd imagined it happening, with a woman he had only known for one night of passion, and with whom had he had no intention of settling down.

Not that Elspeth wanted to settle down either. He'd breathed a sigh of relief over that—the fact that she didn't want a relationship any more than he did. But there was no question that it would make the whole 'practicalities of parenting' thing harder. He had no intention of being an absent father, but he didn't want to live in the city either. Which meant he'd better get used to being in his car, driving in and out of Edinburgh's busy roads on a—what? A weekly trip to see his child?

It wasn't going to be enough, he realised. He didn't want to miss a day of his child's life. He wanted to be there for all of it.

A shudder went through him as he thought about what his father had missed out on when he'd chosen his stepmother over him. All those years he had lost that couldn't be retrieved. Fraser was not going to let that happen to his baby. His child would always know, unquestioningly, that his father loved him. His child would always come first.

At least he and Elspeth saw eye to eye on that one. He thought back to what she had said about her family—her responsibilities. He had to respect the choices she had made. They were the choices he wished his father had made. Choosing family and responsibility over the passion and lust that everyone knew would fade a couple of years into a relationship.

Emotions like that could not and should not be trusted. They certainly shouldn't be the basis of important life decisions.

So why did his mind and his body have to

torment him with reminders of just how much passion and lust he had felt for Elspeth? He was trying to make smart decisions. Trying to do the right thing, But all his brain cared to remind him of was how good it had felt to be with her. How satiated and content he had felt, exhausted and sweaty, with her lying in his arms. How still he had felt in that moment, just holding her close.

But it couldn't happen again. Because he'd seen how the lure of those feelings clouded judgement and screwed up priorities. His only priority now was his child. And that meant that any thoughts of a rematch of that wedding night had to be shelved. If there was one woman in the world that he couldn't have, it was Elspeth.

CHAPTER FOUR

ELSPETH LACED UP her trainers and wondered at what point she would stop being able to tie her own shoes. At just about twelve weeks pregnant her body barely felt any different from before. Her jeans were maybe a little tight, and her breasts a little sore. But the nausea that had coloured the last few weeks was starting to fade, and she could feel a surge of energy building to carry her through the next trimester.

There were no obvious outward signs of the life that was growing inside her, and even her mother hadn't guessed what was going on until she'd confessed all a week or two ago. But now Elspeth was booked in with a midwife and had a scan appointment in a few days. There was no escaping the fact that this baby was real.

She wondered whether Fraser would be able

to see a difference in her and thought back to that night after the wedding, how he had touched her and held her and caressed her. Would he notice the very slight roundness of her belly? The subtle changes in her breasts?

Not that he was getting anywhere near her breasts, she reminded herself. The last thing this situation needed was the complication of a romantic relationship. They had enough to worry about without their feelings getting involved.

Since that morning in the lounge of the hotel they had exchanged a few brief texts, mainly about how the pregnancy was going, and relaying any news about the baby. Other than that there had been nothing said between them that would have given away how intimate they'd been just a few months ago. No hint of the chemistry that she couldn't deny had been seriously hot that night.

The sudden arrival of an enormous muddy black four-by-four beside her broke her train of thought, and she looked up to see Fraser behind the wheel, disconnecting a cable and tapping on his phone so she had a minute to watch him before he realised what she was doing.

The stubble on his jaw looked more than a day old, and his hair was wild and unkempt. He couldn't look more different than he had at the start of that wedding, with his hair dragged straight and under control and a smooth jaw-line. But she suspected that this was closer to the man he really was, with no regard for his hair and mud spattered up the sides of his car.

She smiled, pleased to have been gifted this unguarded moment, and then started as Fraser glanced out of the window and saw her watching. She refused to blush, breathing deep and evenly, forcing her body not to react. It was a trick she'd learnt young, not wanting her pale Celtic skin to give away her every emotion.

Fraser swung down from the car and, remembering their awkwardness the last few times they'd seen each other, Elspeth decided to take the lead and reached up to give him a peck on the cheek. A handshake would have been ridiculous, given everything that had happened between them, and she'd been thinking about how this was going to work.

They needed to be friends. It was important for their baby that they got on with one another. That they worked together to give this child everything it needed. If they couldn't manage a kiss on the cheek, then they were in serious trouble.

'Hi,' she said, trying to make her smile seem natural as she lowered herself from her tiptoes. She'd forgotten how he towered over her. How much she'd loved the feeling of her body being literally overwhelmed by him.

'Hi,' Fraser replied, and for a few moments he didn't move away.

She didn't want to either. She stayed close to him, smiling up, caught in the memory of how good it had felt to have his body tight against hers. How naturally they had read one another, how in sync they had felt that night.

And then Elspeth's smile dropped as she remembered where it had led. The consequences of that intimacy.

Basking in the warm glow of a smile and a physical connection was all well and good if you had no responsibilities. But that wasn't her life—and she had to remember that. The days when she had been able to indulge herself with romantic fantasies were long gone—if they'd ever really existed at all.

She took a deliberate step back, and Fraser seemed to sense her change in mood, his face falling and darkening as she could only assume her own had.

'Are you sure you're up to a walk?' he asked. 'I don't know much about this pregnancy stuff, but I read a couple of books and I'm pretty sure you're meant to take things easy.'

Elspeth couldn't help her smile returning at the thought of him poring over mother and baby manuals.

'I'm fine, really. I'd tell you if it wasn't. We'll take a gentle route up.'

Fraser nodded and looked out over the park, up towards the climb to Arthur's Seat—a jagged rocky peak that towered over the city of Edinburgh, the remains of a long-extinct volcano. 'Do you come and walk up here often?' he asked.

'Not as often as I should,' Elspeth said, realising it was true. 'I suppose it's that thing of stuff being on your doorstep—you forget to do all the things that the guidebooks flog to the tourists.'

Fraser gave an offended snort, digging his hands in his pockets. 'It's not just the tourists, you know. I walk up here whenever I'm in the city.'

'I'm calling you out on not being a tourist,' Elspeth said, clicking the button to lock her car as they walked towards the path leading out of the car park. 'You might not be wearing tartan trousers and touring a distillery, but you're not part of the city—I can tell that much.'

She'd had to go on her instincts, fill in some blanks, she realised, because she knew so little about him. This man had donated fifty per cent of the genetic material she was growing inside her, and yet she didn't know even the most basic things about him.

Time for some digging, she realised. Time to work out who this man was and how she was going to fit him into her life.

'I lived here for a few years when I was a teenager,' Fraser said. 'Before I went back north.'

'That explains the accent, at least.' Elspeth smiled. 'The city's softened it.'

Fraser returned her smile, but it didn't quite reach his eyes. 'You'd make my mother weep.'

'I live to make mothers weep.'

'I like the sound of that.'

She caught his eye and enjoyed the heat in his expression as they stopped and took one another in. It was so easy. Like it had been that night at the wedding, talking with him was so natural. And afterwards, falling into bed with him had been effortless. He'd known everything that she'd wanted. She'd seen everything that he'd needed.

And then she jerked back to the present and self-consciousness set in as she remembered that she shouldn't be thinking of him like that—that the life growing inside her put anything else entirely out of reach.

'What about you?' Fraser asked. 'Edinburgh born and bred?'

'Yep, that's me,' she said, gratefully leaping on the change of subject. 'I've never left the city limits. God, I'm kidding,' she added, when she saw the look of horror on his face. So much for lightening the mood. 'You don't like the city?' she asked.

'Edinburgh's my favourite city. Does that count?'

She narrowed her eyes. 'Well, that kind of depends on what you think of all the others.'

'I don't feel natural in a city.' He shrugged. 'It feels…constraining. I need fresh air. Open spaces.'

Elspeth smiled. That much she'd started to work out for herself. 'So you left as soon as you could?' she guessed. 'College? University?'

He nodded and named a specialist agricultural college near Inverness.

'When you say you're a country boy…'

She found that she was somewhat impressed, though she couldn't put her finger on why. But his commitment to a way of life, to the countryside that he so obviously loved, was commendable. And there was something sexy and grounded about a man who was so connected to the earth.

'I mean there's mud in my veins, rather than blood.'

Elspeth realised that even with as long as they had been talking about what he loved she still had no actual idea what he did for a living.

'So you work in—what? Farming?' she asked, pitching a guess towards the only countryside occupation her city-bred mind could think of.

She knew that she sounded ignorant, but in all honesty she couldn't think of a time in her life when she had even thought about how the countryside worked. That someone had to be out there *making* it work.

'Not really. I had a little money from my grandparents' will when I turned twenty-one, and I invested it in some land I wanted to see developed in a sustainable way. The development made a profit, so I bought more land, built some more properties,' Fraser replied.

Elspeth raised her eyebrows, encouraging him to tell her more.

'Well-developed and well-managed country estates generate an income, which means I can buy more land, which I manage profitably… You can see how it goes.'

'Okay…'

With those titbits of information, and what she'd already seen of where he stayed when he was in Edinburgh, it was becoming increasingly clear how different their lives were. She hadn't given much thought to the luxurious hotel suite he'd taken her back to the night of the wedding. But when he'd suggested the same luxury hotel when she'd met him for a second time she'd guessed that he had money. Serious money.

Great. Money wasn't exactly known to *un*-complicate situations—and what was he going to make of her less than glamorous lifestyle? The nineteen-fifties bungalow that she shared with her mother and her sister? Was his money a part of him that she would ever understand, or would it always be a gulf between them? A part of one another that would always be alien.

It didn't matter, she reminded herself. She didn't want to date him. All she needed from him was to be a good father to their child.

'Are you okay?' Fraser asked, looking at her with concern.

Elspeth waved away his worries and looked out at the view. 'Fine,' she said. 'Just need a breather for a moment.'

She stood looking out over the city and realised how close Fraser was behind her. So close she could practically feel the heat radiating from his chest and his torso. Those tight abs that she'd explored, and then owned, the night of the wedding.

It would be too easy to lean back into him, to let the chemistry that had led them astray that night be back in charge. But it would only lead to trouble, she reminded herself. She was taking on enough with this baby, the baby that was making its presence known by literally stealing the oxygen from her lungs, without trying to make space in her life for a relationship as well.

No, it didn't matter how attracted she was to Fraser. Falling for him meant devoting less of herself to her mother and her sister, and that wasn't an option. Sarah needed her, and Elspeth's feelings came a distant second to that.

She let the breath go and started walking again, determined to reach the top of the hill before they had to turn around, looking for a change of subject. 'Have you told your family about me? About the baby?' she asked, not sure where she wanted this conversation to go, but aware that she needed a change of subject.

'I told my mum,' Fraser said, with a nod and a smile. 'She was pretty shocked, but she's excited about being a grandmother. And desperate to meet you.'

Elspeth grimaced nervously. 'Mine too. My mum, I mean. And my sister. Well, once the shock wore off and they regained the power of speech. What about your dad?' she asked as an afterthought, remembering, as she did sometimes, that most people had more than one parent to consider.

'I've not told my dad, actually,' Fraser said. 'We're not in touch.'

'I'm sorry,' Elspeth said, slipping without thinking about it into her sympathetic doctor's voice. 'Do you want to talk about it?'

'No.' Fraser's tone made it clear that the topic was not up for discussion, and he turned back to the path, picking up his pace. 'What about you?' he asked. 'You mentioned your mum and your sister. Is your dad around?'

She shook her head. 'He never has been.'

Fraser's expression told her exactly what he thought about a father who abandoned his children, and she wondered about his relationship with his dad. How long had it been since they had spoken? What had happened to drive them apart? Was he the reason Fraser bristled as much as she did every time that chemistry sparked between them?

'Probably better that way,' Fraser said.

Well, that was one way to look at it, she thought, surprised at his reaction. But was it really better to have been abandoned by one of her parents? And did she really want to raise a child with someone who thought that way? If she had the choice, two parents seemed like a pretty good deal.

'You know,' Fraser said, his tone still brusque, 'we haven't spoken at all about how this is going to work. I mean, where I'm working now—it's not quite the Highlands, but it's more than an hour from the city. I don't even know where you live. Do you live with your mother?'

Elspeth bristled, wondering whether that was a criticism. 'And my sister. It's not like we have a choice. We all rely on each other.'

'Right. So we're both stuck where we are, and somehow we have to come up with how we give this baby the family that it deserves. And we've got six months—more or less—to figure this out. Shouldn't we be concentrating on that?'

He said it as if it hadn't occupied just about every free moment that she'd had in the last three months. Her shoulders rose as she prepared to defend herself against his implied criticism.

'Brilliant. If you've got this sussed, then I'm all ears.'

'I didn't say that I had the answers,' Fraser snapped. 'Just that we need to start thinking about it.'

'*Start* thinking about it?' Well, if he wasn't going to hold his temper in check, she wasn't either. 'Fraser, I've thought about nothing else since I took that pregnancy test. The fact that I haven't come up with an answer doesn't reflect the amount of effort I've put in.'

'I'm sure you've been thinking about it.' Fraser said, stopping and grabbing her hand so she had no choice but to look him in the eye. 'I have too. But we've not been *talking* about it.

Thinking about this separately isn't the same as thinking about this together.'

He squeezed the hand he was still holding and a jolt of electricity went up her arm—a warning of the danger that still existed just from being close to him. A reminder that if she wanted to keep her head she couldn't get too close.

The sun was behind her. She could feel it warm on the back of her head as the gentle breeze caught at her hair. The sun gleamed off Fraser's hair too, and fine lines appeared around his eyes as he squinted in the bright light. High above the city, in the quiet they had found up here, it was harder to ignore that insistent nagging feeling, the reminder of everything she had felt for him that night. Of how hot their chemistry had been. Of how easily the conversation and the laughs had come.

'I'm not going to be an absent dad,' Fraser said, and the *like my own* was so clear it didn't need to be said out loud.

Elspeth shook her head, glad that he had brought her thoughts back to the baby, where they should be. Not on that night.

'I'm not going to be some bit-part player in my child's life.'

'I don't want that either,' Elspeth admitted. It wasn't going to be easy, having him in her life. Not when her body had its own very firm ideas of what it wanted from him, which were strictly off-limits. But they both owed it to their baby to work out how to be around each other.

'I'll look at my property portfolio,' Fraser said at last. 'See if there's a place in the city that's suitable for us. For me and a room for the baby, I mean. If not, I'll see what's on the market.'

'What about your work?' Elspeth asked.

He shrugged. 'I don't have to be there twenty-four-seven. I can work from the city some of the time if I have to. I'll work it out. This is too important not to.'

Elspeth nodded, and they walked on.

'Are you going to carry on living with your mum?' Fraser asked.

'I don't have a choice,' Elspeth said. 'My mum and I take care of my sister. My sister and I help Mum out. They both help me put in the hours at work that I need to do so that we can pay the mortgage. If I leave, the whole ecosystem stops working.'

Her sister had mentioned once or twice that she would like to move out one day, but Elspeth had been trying to break it to her gently that there was no way it could happen. Elspeth needed to oversee all her care, and it just wouldn't be possible if they weren't under the same roof.

She glanced across and saw Fraser nodding. 'I understand that—sounds like a lot of pressure on you, though. And there's enough room for you all, when the baby gets here?'

'For now.' She nodded, with more confidence than she felt. 'The baby will sleep in my room. And when that's not possible any more…'

Well, I'll cross that bridge when we come to it, she thought.

By the time the baby was born her training post would have finished and she should have been offered a permanent job. Janet was happy enough with her, and the shortage of GPs across the country was in her favour. But… But what if she didn't get the job? What if she couldn't find anything else near her home, so that she would always be nearby if she was needed?

She felt a twinge of anxiety. This was when she was meant to be making big commitments in her career—while her mum was still mobile, before her responsibilities grew even more. She had intended to spend her thirties working every unsociable hour, taking every extra shift, every on-call, covering for colleagues, all to build up a pot of money and goodwill that would be sorely needed when they all needed more help.

She'd never made the conscious decision that she wouldn't have children—she just hadn't thought about where in her plan it might happen. But then Fraser had come along and all her carefully made plans had been worth less than nothing.

'What are you thinking about?' Fraser asked, and Elspeth realised they had been walking in silence for a good ten minutes.

'Work,' she replied, knowing that she was holding back.

'Anything I can help with?'

'Not really.' She shook her head. There was

no point. Fraser couldn't fix this situation any more than she could. 'Just thinking about what I'm going to do when my training post comes to an end if I don't get this job.'

'You'll get it,' he said, with a confidence she had never felt. 'They must love you. You dragged yourself to that wedding...'

She smiled, knowing that he was thinking about the first time they'd met.

'I definitely earned some Brownie points with that.'

Janet had written a touching note in the thank-you card she'd sent after the event, saying how pleased she was that she had been able to come. And no one seemed to have noticed that she'd sneaked out early, so she was winning all round.

'I'll need you to send me your address,' Fraser said after they'd walked on a bit more. 'I'll start looking for somewhere nearby.'

'Nearby?'

So they might bump into each other in the supermarket, or out for a jog? She felt a shiver of apprehension at the realisation of how present Fraser was going to be in her life from here on in. How impossible it was going to be to ignore him. How much of a challenge it was going to be trying to ignore this chemistry between them. He never said his flat in the city would be *close*.

'Doesn't make sense for me to get a place if it takes me an hour to travel across from the other side of the city.'

'I know. I just hadn't thought…'

'What? That I'd be a part of your life?'

Ugh, she could do without him reading her mind right now.

'I think this is how it works from now on. We have to get used to that.'

Of course he was right. It was just that it had been easy to kid herself so far that nothing was going to change that much. Sure, she'd have a baby to care for, but her whole day was already spent caring for people.

There would be maternity leave, and then, if everything went as she hoped, she would be back at work, just with extra drop-offs and pick-ups to work into her day. Appointments with health visitors and childminders and looking for a nursery. A whole new column to add to her calendar and her diary and her to-do list.

That was the choice she had made. But at no point had she chosen Fraser. Well, she had, she supposed, in the half-light of the botanic gardens. But she'd chosen him for *right then*. For *pleasure*. For *that night*. Not for ever.

'I'm not going to disappear on you or the bairn, Elspeth. Like your dad or mine. I'm here. I'm always going to be here.'

Well, he didn't have to make it sound like a threat... But she felt his words in the pit of her stomach, the commitment that he had just made to her child, and a tiny part of her fear melted away with it.

And then another, larger part, doubled in size. She knew she was never going to be rid of him, and she was going to have to spend her whole lifetime resisting him. It was going to be exhausting, and she had no idea where she was going to find the energy to do it.

'Your dad...' Elspeth started, not really sure where she wanted the conversation to go, just knowing that she wanted it to move away from her, and the changes to her life. He could sit under the spotlight for a while. 'You said that he left. What happened?'

Fraser made a casual gesture, but she could see from the hard-set lines of his face that he felt anything but relaxed about the subject.

'He met someone else. I was fifteen. He and Mum broke up and I told him that if he married the new woman I wouldn't see him again. He chose her.'

Elspeth stopped in her tracks. 'You gave him an ultimatum?'

'And he chose her.'

She stood and looked at him for a moment, shocked by the strength of mind that he'd had at fifteen. The stubbornness that she knew he still had now. 'I'm sorry, Fraser, that must have been hard. And you've had no contact since?'

'He contacts my mum occasionally. But other than that… Nothing.'

She really didn't want to be on the wrong side of an argument with him. This was brutal, she thought, on both sides. Though she couldn't help but consider that his father had been put in an impossible position. There were rarely any winners when people started dishing out ultimatums. But Fraser had only been a kid himself at the time.

'How did your mum feel about this?' Elspeth asked, still trying to imagine the shockwaves that something like this would send through a family.

'She was devastated when he told her he wanted a divorce. It took her years to be happy again. I couldn't see him after watching her go through that. And I couldn't go back to… I couldn't go home. To see someone else in our home. He destroyed our family.'

'But surely…?'

Elspeth hesitated. She knew that she didn't have all the information, but to cut off any contact like that seemed so…*drastic*. It was heartbreaking when a family broke up, but plenty of people managed to keep relationships going in worse circumstances. People less stubborn than Fraser and his father, clearly.

'You don't think that was a little…?'

The look on Fraser's face told her that her opinion was not welcome on this subject. Well, fine. Not today. But she had a feeling that they would be revisiting this one.

'I suppose I'll have to see him now, though,' Fraser said eventually, and Elspeth whipped her head round to look at him.

'Why?' she asked. 'I mean, I'm all for it, if my opinion counts for anything,' she clarified.

The last thing she wanted was her baby to be born in the middle of a family feud, but this was such an about-turn. After what—fifteen years of silence?—he was suddenly going to change his mind?

'Because my father still lives in our family home. It's a part of me, and I want my child to know it. That's more important than how I feel about my father.'

She gave him a sidelong look, aware that there was something she wasn't understanding here, that Fraser was choosing to hold back.

She felt a shot of something cold. A protective instinct that she recognised as maternal. The first stirrings of her inner mama bear. 'The baby's home will be with us,' she said.

'Of course with us. But it's also...*there*. Where I grew up.'

Elspeth bit her tongue. It was as clear as anything that Fraser was still carrying a lot of emotional baggage about his father. But it wasn't her place to interfere. She wasn't his wife, or even his girlfriend. She was the mother of his child, and that was it. No opinions about his personal life were allowed. Or necessary, she remembered. This wasn't her fight, however sad she might be for that poor teenaged Fraser, feeling abandoned by his dad.

'Well, I can be there with you. If you want,' Elspeth said.

Fraser caught at her hand and gave it a squeeze. 'Thanks.'

She snatched her fingers back, surprised at the heat she had felt zipping from his hand to hers. The last thing she needed was to be reminded of that.

Fraser looked at her, his eyes narrowed as he took in her reaction. 'I was just saying thanks,' he said, raising his hands in a show of innocence. 'It didn't mean anything.'

'I know that. But it's just… I don't want things to get confusing.'

Fraser narrowed his eyes. 'Confusing how?'

She took a step back, needing to put some space between them. 'Confusing like thinking that it would be a good idea for something to happen between us.'

'All I did was hold your hand.' He shook his head.

'I know that. But it reminded me…'

It had reminded her of every skin-on-skin second they had shared before, and it had made her body crave more. And that couldn't happen. She couldn't allow herself to think like that. To want that. It was too dangerous. She fought to keep her body neutral. To quieten her pulse, to fight the rush of blood to her face. She was an adult, and she was in control of her body. Her decisions. Her desires.

'It doesn't matter what it reminded me of,' she told Fraser eventually, her voice admirably calm. 'I just want to be clear about what's on offer here and what's…*not*.'

'I think you're making that very clear,' Fraser said.

She searched his face and his voice for any hint of annoyance but couldn't find one. He seemed irritatingly nonchalant about the whole thing, if she was honest. Was she pleased about that? Was this easy for him? Did he not think about it at *all*?

She needed to make sure that he completely understood, though. Given how they had met, and all the changes in their lives since then, she had to make sure that they were on the same page when it came to their relationship. Had to make sure that he understood that they could only ever be friends. Anything else was too complicated.

'I think we need to acknowledge that there is chemistry between us. I mean, that's what got us here, isn't it? But we can't act on it any more. We can't be tempted. We need to be good parents to this baby. We need to be thinking straight. Making sensible decisions. We can't be getting distracted by whatever feelings we had for each other that night.'

He quirked the corner of his lip in an annoying hint of a smile, as if he was finding this whole conversation amusing rather than embarrassing. 'And what feelings *did* you have for me that night?'

Oh, she could have listed them: lust, desire, need, abandon, *want*. But someone had to be the responsible one here, so instead, she shook her head.

'We're not talking about that night. We're talking about now. And right now the only feelings I have for you are friendly. We are going to be friends. We are going to raise this child together. And we are never going to talk about that night again.'

'Never talk about it again? Might that not get awkward?'

He shrugged and she decided that, yes, his nonchalance was *definitely* annoying. 'Why would it be awkward?'

'People are going to have questions,' Fraser replied. 'Our friends. Our families. They're going to want to know what's happening with us.'

'Oh, and you usually spill all about your sex life to your friends and your family, do you?'

'No, but there's a baby on the way…'

She nodded emphatically and started walking again. 'Exactly. That tells them all they need to know about what has happened in the past. When they want to know what's happening with us now, we tell them the truth. That we're friends.'

Fraser fell silent, obviously thinking that through. 'You know, we never considered the alternative.'

For the first time she heard a shake in his voice, heard doubt in his tone.

'We've never talked about doing the right thing. Marrying. Making a proper family for this baby.'

Elspeth wasn't sure whether she was meant to laugh or not. That was the most unromantic proposal of marriage she had ever heard, and from the look on Fraser's face he'd dragged it out like needles through his skin. She was tempted to accept, just to see the look of horror on his face, but even she wasn't that cruel.

'Is that what you really want for our family, Fraser? The two of us pretending to be something we're not because we think it's the right thing for the baby?'

He looked relieved that she hadn't said yes, but aware that she hadn't said no either. She had no intention of doing so—she was more interested in exploring the reasons he'd asked in the first place.

'Aren't we meant to be putting the baby's needs first?' he asked, tiptoeing his way through the words.

'Why does that have to mean marriage? Your mum and mine have both done fine on their own.'

'But you're not on your own. You've got me; I'm not going anywhere.'

Elspeth crossed her arms. 'Exactly, so we don't need a marriage certificate to tell us that. Your name will be on the birth certificate, and that's enough for me.'

'You're not interested in the whole nuclear family thing?'

'I guess not.'

'What about when you meet someone else?'

The thought hadn't even occurred to her. It was hard enough accepting that she was going to have to make room in her life for Fraser and their child. The thought that she might meet someone else one day, make room for them too—it was laughable. She'd tried once before to make a relationship work with the other commitments in her life, and it had threatened to take her away from her sister. The person who needed her more than anyone. She wouldn't be making that decision again—not with him or with anyone else.

She thought back to the night she'd spent with Fraser, how they'd clicked from their first banter at the wedding to her first orgasm, to that first and last kiss of the morning when she'd sneaked out of his hotel room. If she couldn't find a way to make a relationship work with that kind of incentive, she didn't much fancy anyone else's chances.

'I don't want anybody else.'

It was easier to say that than to tell the truth. How would Fraser, with his money and his privilege, understand the compromises and the struggles that were an everyday part of her life? How was he going to react when she didn't finish work until long after she wanted to be in bed because the practice was overstretched and her patients needed her attention? When her mum had been in so much pain after work that she'd had to go straight to bed and so there were dishes and laundry to do? When her sister needed her? When her mother could no longer look after herself?

Alex had made it clear that it wasn't something you signed up for voluntarily.

There was no point pretending that she was looking forward to a life without romance, but some things took priority. If she had to choose—again—she'd make the same decision every time. Nothing would ever be more important to her than her family.

As they reached the top of Arthur's Seat she took a moment to look at the view, seeing the whole of the city spread out beneath them and realising how high they'd climbed. She was a little out of breath—no doubt courtesy of the baby now sharing her oxygen and blood supply.

But, having climbed up here with Fraser, she was sure of one thing. They were going to fight for this. Probably with each other at times, but hopefully on the same team too. They were going to be a family. They would make it work because they both loved this baby.

The fact that they didn't love each other wouldn't change that.

CHAPTER FIVE

WHEN FRASER HAD suggested grabbing something to eat after the twelve-week scan she hadn't realised that he'd meant *here.* She had shoes she'd be happy to wear to a Michelin-starred restaurant in one of the city's most exclusive hotels, but she didn't usually throw them on when she was expecting to go for a scan and then straight back home. And catching sight of her battered old trainers was making her mightily uncomfortable.

The interior of the restaurant was opulently decorated, and the pale September sun that braved it past the heavy velvet curtains and dark wooden panelling glinted on the crystal glasses and the chandeliers above them. She couldn't remember the last time she'd been in this part of the city, and she'd forgotten how packed the Royal Mile could be with visitors—even outside of the usual touristy times of year.

She would walk back through the closes and wynds, she promised herself, thinking of the quiet alleyways that snaked through the Old Town, down the steep hill towards the New Town and away from the main thoroughfare. No matter how familiar she was with the city she still found something new to see every time, looking up towards the sky at the teetering buildings, five or six storeys above the narrow cobbled passageways below.

The wait staff were hovering at the edges of the room, and she remembered that she was meant to be choosing something to order. The food looked incredible—all Aberdeen Angus steak and oozing egg yolks and local game—normally everything she could have wanted from a menu. But with pregnancy safety advice in the forefront of her mind after the scan she couldn't see a single thing that looked both safe to eat and appealing.

Fraser didn't seem to care that neither of them was dressed for a fancy lunch, and was still wearing the blissed-out expression that he had adopted when the sonographer had drizzled the cold gel on her belly, touched the probe to her skin and showed them their baby's flickering heartbeat just a second later.

Elspeth looked up from her menu and smiled across the table at Fraser. Seeing their baby on the screen had been a breathtaking moment, and she was so glad they had shared it together. At her first scan—when she'd gone alone, not sure whether this baby was going to have one parent or two, half convinced that she'd completely imagined seeing the word 'pregnant' on the test she'd taken a few weeks before—there had been nothing more than a tiny pulsing flicker.

But this time they had seen her baby—their baby—with its tiny arms and legs and fingers. Fraser had gripped her hand, and in that moment she'd known that it didn't matter how this baby had come about. They were both going to love it with an intensity that threatened to suffocate her.

But now they had left that little bubble, and the real world was creeping back in.

'I can't believe we saw our baby,' she said, for about the hundredth time since they'd left the hospital, trying to recapture their mood in the hospital.

'Pretty amazing,' Fraser said, nodding. 'When do we get to see him again?' he asked.

'Easy with the *him* stuff,' Elspeth reminded him. 'We don't know the sex yet. And the next scan is at twenty weeks. We can find out the sex then, if we want to.'

Fraser's eyebrows shot up. 'Not for another two months? What if something goes wrong before then?'

Elspeth bristled, sitting up a little straighter. 'Why would anything go wrong?'

'I'm not saying it will,' Fraser said. 'But it's a long time between scans. I want the baby to be checked more often.'

She shook her head. Here spoke a man with little experience of the NHS and none of pregnancy.

'Well, with most pregnancies there's no need to be seen more often,' she explained, as she would to any patient. 'Everything is fine.'

'But in some pregnancies there *are* problems, and I don't want us to be one of those pregnancies,' Fraser pressed on, seemingly unaware that her hackles were rapidly rising. 'As soon as we're done here I'm going to get us booked in to the private hospital. I want the best for you both, and waiting two months for another scan can't be the best.'

'And you're basing this on what?' Elspeth asked, her voice tart, annoyed at his high-handed tone. 'Your extensive obstetric knowledge?'

Was he really suggesting that she wouldn't do what was right for their baby? That she would cut corners to save money? *She* was the one who actually knew what she was talking about when it came to the medical side of things. She wasn't going to let him have his own way just because he wanted to throw his money and his privilege around.

'I just don't see why we wouldn't pay for extra care for our baby,' he said, laying down his menu and glaring at her.

Elspeth tried to tamp down her temper before she spoke, but she was finding it more and more difficult. 'This isn't a situation that you just throw money at, Fraser. You weigh up the costs and benefits of additional investigations. I don't see the need for more.'

Fraser took a sip of his drink and shrugged. 'I don't see the downside. I'm not going to change my mind.'

'Really? You surprise me.' Forget keeping her temper—it wasn't *her* fault he was being completely illogical. 'Well, with my five years of medical school, and seven more of training, I *might* have picked up something about weighing up the risks and benefits of additional testing in a medical setting. But if you think your gut feeling and your bank balance outweigh that experience—'

He held his hands up. 'Fine. If you feel so strongly, stay at your hospital—don't bother with the extra scans. But I'm not going to pretend that I understand. I think you're making a mistake.'

Too right he didn't understand. And if he wanted to go private now, when they'd had a textbook visit, with a ten-minute wait in a comfortable room and a friendly sonographer who had chatted as she'd talked them through the scan, what was he going to make of her family's regular middle-of-the-night trips to the emergency department? Of dealing with underfunded community services and appointments cancelled and moved at the last minute? The sort of things that made up most of the days of her life. And that was when she wasn't working extra shifts to cover their understaffed and underfunded GP practice…

'What?' he asked, and she guessed that some of what she was thinking must be showing on her face.

'Nothing…' she hedged. 'I was just thinking how different we are. How different our lives are. Wondering how this is going to work.'

'I don't think we're that different,' he countered, leaning forward on his elbows and fixing her with a look.

'You think this is the sort of place to come for a quick lunch,' she stated, glancing around her.

He drew his eyebrows together and frowned. 'I thought you'd like it. I mean, it's not where I usually come in my walking boots and my waterproof jacket.'

'Right—Fraser the country boy.'

He narrowed his eyes. 'I'll choose not to take that as an insult.'

'It wasn't.' She lifted her hands, not sure how to get across what she was thinking. 'But we're *different*. I love this city. You're clearly uncomfortable here. You'd rather be out at one of your estates—and when I say "estate" we both know I'm not talking about new-build semis,' she clarified. 'My life is spent in city hospitals like the one you thought wasn't good enough today, and you've spent the last week looking to acquire—what? A…a stately home?'

'A castle.'

'A castle? Right. And you're buying it from…?'

'A duke.'

Elspeth nodded—he had just proved her point. Even if her family didn't present its own challenges, they were too different. Their lives were too different for this ever to be anything other than impossible.

'A duke is just a person,' Fraser said, holding her gaze, not letting her look away. 'No different from anyone else.'

'Yeah, right. Castles notwithstanding.'

Elspeth watched Fraser as a cloud crossed his face.

'I'm serious. Titles don't mean anything,' he said.

Elspeth stopped and gave him a long look. 'You're taking this rather personally.'

He nodded. 'I have reason to.'

'You have a…a title?' Elspeth asked, noting the strain in her own voice.

'A courtesy title—at least while my father's still alive. When he dies I'll inherit the estate and the title that goes with it.'

She took in a deep breath, collecting herself, trying to keep a rein on her thoughts.

How could he have kept this from her? She didn't care about his title. About where he'd grown up and who his family were. But this was *her* baby he was talking about. She had seen him or her on the screen that afternoon, waving at them with its perfect, tiny little fingers. And now Fraser had dropped this bombshell, telling her that her baby was part of something that she could barely understand, never mind be a part of.

'And you're only thinking to mention this

now?' she said, aware that her shock was making her words sharp. 'You didn't say a word about it when we talked about your dad.'

Fraser shrugged and held up his hands. 'It's not usually my opening gambit when I'm picking up women.'

'Wow—and doesn't *that* make me feel special?'

She glanced down at the menu again, using it as a handy way to hide her face. At least Fraser had made it very clear where she stood, she supposed. She was just some woman he had picked up—one of many, by the sounds of it. If there hadn't been a baby they never would have seen each other again.

'I imagine a castle and a title have a pretty high success rate,' she said, when she was sure she could speak calmly, determined to show him she didn't care that she had been nothing more than a one-night stand to him. That was all he had been to her as well, after all.

Fraser snorted, pouring them both a glass of water. 'Evidently not with you,' he said. 'You seem pretty annoyed about it, actually.'

Well, he was observant enough—she would give him that.

'I am *pretty annoyed* about the fact that you haven't mentioned it before. This is the sort of thing I think I should know about the father of my child. When were you planning on telling me?'

'I didn't really have a plan,' Fraser said.

He really wasn't helping himself here. Still, he was making it easier and easier for her to remember that under no circumstances should she be thinking about having a relationship with him.

'You were going to hide it from me?' she asked.

'That's not the same thing.'

'I don't even know what to call you,' she said at last, her frustration getting the better of her. 'Am I meant to curtsey?'

Fraser gave a frustrated bark of laughter. 'You call me Fraser, just like before. And don't be angry.' He reached across to brush the gentlest of touches against her fingertips, where she was clutching her water glass with a death grip. 'This isn't about you or the baby,' he continued. 'I don't like to talk about my family because it's complicated.'

'Well, I'm family now too. I think we should talk about this.'

He drew away, rested back in his chair and gave her a long look. 'I'm not sure what to tell you, apart from what you already know. I've not seen my father or been back to our estate since I was a teenager,' Fraser said after a few moments.

'So you're buying all this land, these other estates…?'

'Because I can't go back to my own.' Fraser nodded slowly, thoughtfully. 'I wish I could. I miss it like—'

Fraser cut himself off and took a long sip of his water. Elspeth kept her eyes on him, waiting until he was ready to speak again.

'Thank you,' she said. 'For sharing it with me now. I want us to be able to talk.'

He reached for her hand. 'I still can't believe we saw him,' he said, throwing a glance to a waiter, who had appeared beside them with a tray and two champagne flutes. 'It's nonalcoholic,' Fraser said, reading her mind. 'But I thought we should have a toast.'

She smiled. He was right. This wasn't about them. This was about doing what was right for their baby. Their feelings for one another didn't have to come into it at all.

'To the baby,' she said, clinking her glass against his and taking a sip.

But just because she had let this conversation rest for now, that didn't mean it was over. There was still so much that they didn't understand about one another's lives, and she wasn't sure how they were ever going to reconcile that. There was a part of him, and of her child now, that would always feel like a stranger to her.

CHAPTER SIX

'Is it going to be big enough?' Fraser asked a few weeks later, as they viewed an apartment in Edinburgh's exclusive West End.

Big enough? She looked around the room that she was standing in. The floor-to-ceiling windows flooded the old Regency room with light, which reflected back at her from the gilt work on the ceiling, the white marble of the enormous fireplace, the top of the grand piano and the polished floorboards beneath her feet.

You could have fitted her family's whole semi-detached bungalow into this one room. Okay, maybe she was exaggerating a little—but only a little. When Fraser had said that he was going to find an apartment in the city, she'd envisaged a two-bedroomed bachelor flat, just a room for him and a nursery for the baby. Not this luxury.

She was reminded once again of how different their lives were. How their homes would always look so different. His filled with designer furnishings and a grand piano, just 'because', and hers with medical equipment and stray stethoscopes.

'It's plenty big enough,' she said with a slightly brittle laugh. 'How big do you think this baby is going to be?'

'Ah, but I've done my research,' Fraser said, smiling and pointing a finger in the general direction of her newly apparent baby bump. 'A baby equals about seven or eight pounds and twenty inches long. The *stuff* that comes with one is approximately the size and mass of the Milky Way.'

Elspeth laughed again—properly this time. 'Well, I guess that depends on how much stuff you buy. Me and my mum and my sister manage in somewhere half the size of this, and we come with about thirty years' worth of accumulated junk and a shedload of medical equipment.'

Fraser's face fell, and she guessed he was only just starting to see how different the experiences they brought to this relationship were.

'But wouldn't you want more space if it were an option? Would you just "manage" if you didn't have to?'

'I'm not good with hypotheticals,' Elspeth said, any trace of laughter gone from her voice. Was he judging her? For having less money? A smaller house than he did?

'Okay,' he said. 'Let's make this less hypothetical.'

Fraser spoke quickly, and she wondered how much of her annoyance had shown on her face.

'This baby is going to have a lot of money at his or her disposal. I think we ought to talk about how we're going to approach that.'

Elspeth crossed her arms. Still wondering whether he was criticising. Judging. 'I don't want to raise a spoiled brat.'

Fraser raised an eyebrow. 'And do *I* fall into that category?'

Elspeth shrugged. 'I never said that.' *Out loud.*

'But you know that I was raised with money. Do you think it's made me a bad person? Am I a brat?'

Well, if he was going to ask a leading question…

'You know what you want,' she replied, not directly answering his question. 'You're good at getting it. You *expect* to get it.'

He oozed confidence and privilege with an ease that made it apparent he didn't realise he was doing it. It wasn't his fault. He couldn't help the position he'd been born into any more than anyone else could. But that didn't mean he should be ignorant of it.

'I'm not sure I should apologise for that,' he said.

She didn't point out that she'd never asked him to. They both knew her criticism had been implied.

'It's just not what I'm used to,' Elspeth said, trying to be conciliatory. 'I'm sure we'll find a middle ground.'

'I want to make sure that my child is provided for.'

'And I'm not capable of doing that?' Being conciliatory didn't extend to ignoring his criticism of how she took care of her family.

'I just don't see why you don't want me to

spend the money I've worked hard to make on our bairn.'

She smiled, unable to help herself, at the words 'our bairn' from his lips. From the look on his face as he'd said it.

'Let me look after both of you,' he continued, sitting back on the arm of the nearest sofa, his body language relaxed and open. 'All three of us.'

Reluctantly, she smiled and nodded, intoxicated by the sight of Fraser in his new role as doting dad. She sat in the armchair beside him, tucking her feet underneath her.

'You know, we've never really talked much about your family,' Fraser went on. 'Tell me more about caring for your sister. How is it with the three of you living together?'

'It's the only arrangement that makes sense. I do as much of Sarah's care as I can myself. Sarah's mentioned getting her own place, but I don't think she really appreciates what that would mean. More care from strangers…less from me and Mum. I hate the thought of it.'

'And did your ex live with you too?' Fraser asked, throwing her a curveball by mentioning Alex.

She shook her head. 'No. In fact we called things off when it became clear that it wasn't going to work for him. And he was right. We never stood a chance—not with all the other responsibilities I have in my life. He would always have had to share me with my family. It wasn't fair on him.'

'I'm starting to think he didn't deserve you,' Fraser said. 'But tell me more about caring for your sister,' he added, looking genuinely interested. 'I want to understand what your life is like.'

She didn't bother correcting him about Alex. She had been right to call things off. But Fraser had asked about Sarah, and she smiled, much happier talking about her sister than her failed attempt at being a fiancée.

'My whole job is to make sure she can do whatever she needs to and to help her do as much for herself as she can manage. A lot of it is pretty basic: cutting up food, making drinks, driving her to medical appointments. Then there's the more specialised stuff, like physio, her medication—that sort of thing. She's stubborn and fierce and independent, so I'm just there to fill in the gaps when she can't do something she wants to. She was born when I was twelve; I've helped to care for her all my adult life, so I don't really know things any other way and nor does she.'

Fraser smiled. 'Sounds like you two are quite the team. Do you have outside help?'

Elspeth shrugged. 'Only in an emergency. Why would we have someone else in when we are such a good team?'

'It would give you more time,' Fraser suggested gently.

'I don't *want* time. Not if it means compromises for Sarah.'

'You love her very much,' he said plainly. 'I can't wait to see you love our baby like that.'

She met his eyes, and for a second they held each other's gaze, feeling all the potential of a future life, their future family, between them.

'I'll get in touch with my lawyer, then. Start sorting out some paperwork for our finances.'

Elspeth sat back, dropping her feet to the floor and straightening her spine, surprised by his change of direction. 'Lawyers? We're at *lawyers*? What happened to "We'll find a middle ground"? I thought we were working this out ourselves?'

'We will. We are—of course we are. But I want the baby to have security. For ever. I want you to know that whatever happens you'll be provided for.'

'Well, there's nothing melodramatic in *that* sentence to terrify me,' Elspeth replied, taking a step away from him.

What was he planning on happening? Was he creating an escape plan for himself?

'I'm not being melodramatic.' Fraser's voice was darker now. Serious. 'I'm being practical. Families break up. Parents make mistakes. I just want to know that our baby is always going to be taken care of.'

Her instinct was to bite back, to remind him that he was going absolutely nowhere and neither was she. They were going to raise this baby together, just as they had agreed. But then she remembered the look in his eyes when he had spoken about his father. That sad, confused teenager he had been was still just under the surface, still didn't understand why his relationship with his father had broken down, and she decided not to push it.

This conversation was just a symptom of a deeper problem. And the only way to deal with that was for Fraser to come to terms with what had happened between him and his dad.

She thought about the money too. Thought about the years of medical costs and on-call shifts and waiting for payday ahead of her. Knowing that at least her baby would be well provided for had relieved her of a pressure she hadn't even realised she was feeling.

'You're right. Have your lawyer do whatever you think is necessary.' She waited a beat and then asked, 'Have you thought any more about your dad?'

Fraser shot her a dark look, but she decided to press on. She and Fraser didn't know each other that well, but it was clear that his relationship with his father was going to affect his relationship with their child. She didn't want this baby born into conflict or uncertainty—if there was confrontation to be had, it would have to happen before the baby arrived.

'About going to see him?' she added, when Fraser stayed silent.

'It's complicated,' he replied, as if that was an end of the matter.

'Of course it is. That's why if it's going to happen I think it's best to do it well before the baby is here. The last thing we need is to be trekking up to the Highlands when I'm nine months gone.'

'We?'

Elspeth felt her cheeks colour. She'd assumed that she would be going with him. This was all about the baby, after all. And it wasn't as if the baby could go up there without her right now. But obviously Fraser hadn't been planning on introducing her to his family yet. Oh, well, she was too far into this thing to succumb to embarrassment now.

'Yes, *we*,' she said. 'I thought you wanted your dad to know about the baby?'

'I know I have to tell him about it. I thought I'd call him. He's not exactly going to demand to see the evidence. I'm not going up there and you don't have to either, Elspeth. It's going to be…awkward.'

'Of course it is. That's why I'm offering to be your wingman. Wing-woman. Whatever.'

She strengthened her resolve. He needed her there. This was going to be a hideously awkward family reunion, and a neutral observer would keep things on track.

'This is not the sort of conversation you have on the phone. I think you should just go up there and get it done. I'll come with you.'

'Really? You'd do that? Walk smack-bang into the middle of someone else's family drama?'

She shrugged. 'Well, I think *we're* family now. Your family drama is my family drama. And in my experience awkward family stuff usually goes better if you have a drinking partner.'

At last he cracked a smile. 'You're not going to be much use on *that* front.'

Elspeth threw up her hands and laughed softly, relieved that the tension in the room had broken. 'I will happily drink cups of tea while feeding you whisky and mopping up your tears.'

'Well, *that's* a definition of love if ever I heard one.'

Elspeth laughed again, but couldn't deny to

herself the warm glow of something that she felt in the pit of her stomach. Fraser was right. That was family. That was friendship. Wanting to sit with someone and share their pain. To offer support through something difficult even when you stood to gain nothing. That was what you did for someone that you loved. She'd do it unquestioningly for her mother and Sarah. For a handful of her friends. And now, it seemed, for Fraser.

Friendly love. Family love. That was what he had meant. Not *love* love. He didn't think she *loved* him. And she absolutely didn't—she was quite sure about that. But just the mention of the L word had done something to the atmosphere in the room.

The sun had set while they had been talking, and the lamps placed around the room now seemed more mood lighting than bright and welcoming. The soft throw rugs on the white sofa looked sensuous and inviting, and the candle burning on the mantel seemed romantic rather than staged to sell a house.

Suddenly she was standing too close to him, and yet not close enough. Before she realised what she was doing she had taken half a step forward, and he had done the same. Leaving only the space of a breath between her face and his chest.

Elspeth looked up, surprised all over again by how he towered above her, and she felt a shiver of desire as she remembered what it was to be dominated by him. How it had felt to be with him…how aware she had been of his height, his size…how powerful she had felt giving up control to him.

His hand landed on the small of her back at the same moment that her fingertips brushed against his chest, and she had a split second to decide whether she was pulling him closer or pushing him away. Her body swayed towards him, leaving her in no doubt about where her baser instincts wanted her to take this. But reason won out at the last moment and she held her breath, pressing gently against Fraser's chest as she retraced her steps, putting some much-needed space between them.

'I like the apartment,' she said, aware of how inane the words sounded given what had just almost happened between them.

She looked up, curious to see how Fraser would take the change of direction. He raised an eyebrow, and that tiny gesture showed her that he knew exactly what had just nearly happened between them, and that he had seen her swerve perfectly clearly. But he let it lie, and she figured he was as relieved as she was that they hadn't complicated things by giving in to a momentary spike of lust.

They had been perfectly clear with one another that nothing like that was on the cards between them. They just had to be sure to remember it when they were tempted.

'I'll take it, then,' Fraser said.

It took Elspeth a moment to remember that he was talking about the apartment. And then another to marvel at the fact that he could make the decision just like that on a property purchase that must run into seven figures. And then she took *another* moment to remember that this was the life her child was being born into. Would it feel normal for her child, one day, to drop upwards of a million pounds on a second home just because it was more convenient than the castle out in the country where it normally resided?

No, she reminded herself. Because regardless of where Fraser had been born, and regardless of whether he patched things up with his father, this baby would be living with *her*. Her and her mother and Sarah, in their comfortable bungalow with only a few decades of memories and zero coats of arms on the walls.

'We've not even seen all of it yet,' she reminded him.

Though, on reflection, reminding him that they hadn't seen the bedrooms maybe wasn't her most sensible move. He stood back, gesturing her towards the hallway from where several doorways led off. She tried not to feel self-conscious as she walked ahead of him. Tried not to wonder whether he was looking at her bottom in the close-fitting shift dress she had chosen to wear that morning.

It had seemed sensible and professional when she had chosen it. Now it seemed sensuous. She knew that it made the most of the few curves she had, and she couldn't help but wonder whether Fraser had noticed. Had that been what was really on her mind when she had taken it off the hanger a few hours before?

She opened the first door she came to and gave the opulent bathroom a nod. It was big, luxurious and marble. Exactly what she'd expect of a bathroom in an apartment in this part of town. The next door revealed a bedroom, its enormous bed piled high with more pillows, blankets, bedspreads and throws than a bachelor could ever need.

She had a brief thought, not quite fully formed, that this would be where Fraser would sleep—and that he wouldn't always do so alone—and shut the door. Both on the thought and on the bed.

She caught Fraser's eye, and knew that he had clocked something but decided not to say anything. Wise man.

She opened the next door, prepared just to glance inside and then close it as quickly, but the sight of an enormous white cot-bed made her pause with her hand still on the doorknob, temporarily winded.

'Wow…' The sound fell out of her mouth,

barely a word, and she found she didn't have any more to follow it.

She couldn't look away from the cot. The changing table. The tiny wardrobe and the baskets stuffed with toys. This was where her baby would sleep. This was where they would change her or dress him. Rock her to sleep in the chair by the window. Would he learn to crawl on the plush rug in front of the fireplace?

It took her a few moments more to remember that she had the picture all wrong. Her baby might sleep here sometimes. Fraser might change him or her on that table. Might see first steps on that rug. But *she* wouldn't be here. This was where her baby would live when she didn't live with her.

A pain spiked at Elspeth as the knowledge that they were far from a perfectly nuclear family struck her afresh.

Her child would have two homes. It wasn't the worst thing that could happen to a child. Not least because it meant that it would have two parents who were completely devoted to it. But not to each other. There would always be hard choices. Awkward Christmases and long holidays without one parent or the other.

Elspeth reminded herself again of all the ways her baby was lucky. All the incredible advantages he or she would have in life. But she couldn't help feel a little sad that this unconventional but oh, so practical parenting arrangement meant that a lot of the time one parent or the other would be conspicuous by their absence.

'What are you thinking?' Fraser asked.

She didn't know how to put into words everything that was racing through her mind. She realised that all her life she'd had an idea of how family life should be. Some dreamy half-formed image of breakfast in bed and acres of white bedding and a husband beside her. And now that she was expecting a baby, and part of that picture was coming true, the rest of it seemed further away than ever before.

'Just that our baby will sleep here,' she said eventually, filtering her thoughts down to their simplest component part. 'It feels weird,' she added, in case he hadn't picked up on the vibe in the room.

'Yeah,' Fraser added.

She could hear the wonder in his voice. Maybe he wasn't completely oblivious, after all.

'Do you like the room the way it is? I can ask them to leave everything?'

'I think it's gorgeous. Perfect.'

'You don't want to put your own stamp on it?'

'It's *your* home, Fraser...'

Perhaps he hadn't quite reached the same conclusions she had yet. Perhaps it hadn't occurred to him that their family was going to be stretched across at least two homes. That this little picture of familial bliss that the show home had created wasn't really going to apply for them.

'I know, but it's our baby. I want you to be happy with it too.'

'Honestly, it's lovely. Leave it just as it is.'

The atmosphere in the nursery was suddenly stifling, and Elspeth turned for the door. Fraser reached for her hand and she let him take hold of her fingers, but didn't let it stop her leaving. She needed to be out of that room.

As they reached the living room she glanced down at their still clasped hands and Fraser followed her gaze, as if he hadn't realised what he had done. He pulled his hand away, a little more quickly than was comfortable for her ego.

'So, my dad…' Fraser said. 'You're right. We should go. And soon. I'll have to call him.'

Just like that? As if they hadn't been estranged for fifteen years?

'Well, just let me know when. Like I said, I'll be there if you want me.'

Fraser looked again at the number in his phone. Would it even still work? No one he knew answered their landline any more. But it was the only number he had for his dad. He didn't even know why he'd bothered to programme it into his phone. The number was ingrained in his memory, in his childhood—in that part of his life before he'd had a mobile phone, before his family had been torn apart.

He could ask his mum if she had a mobile number for him. He knew that they had been in touch over the years. He'd seen the evidence in his mum's red eyes whenever letters from the family solicitor had arrived on the mat at home. Worst of all had been the time they had found out that his father's second marriage had ended. Every time his father had made his mum cry, Fraser had sworn again that he wouldn't go back. He would never speak to him again.

What would his mum say if she knew that he was thinking of getting in touch with him?

The betrayal would undoubtedly hurt her. She'd been delighted when he'd told her about the baby, and had hardly batted an eyelid at the fact that he wasn't in a relationship with Elspeth. Had she guessed that he would want to go back to Ballanross? She hadn't said a word about it if she had. She'd never told him that she didn't want him to speak to his father. Hadn't had to when he had been able to see the pain that even the mention of his name caused her.

If ever he'd needed a reminder of what following lust and impulsive attraction did to a family it was now. *This* was why he wasn't going to give in to the feelings he had for Elspeth. *This* was why he was going to resist the fact that he wanted her with every bone in his body. Because he wouldn't subject his child to the pain that he and his mother had gone through.

But he couldn't deny his child Ballanross either. As formative as his parents' separation had been, Ballanross had been more so. That feeling of being connected to the land. Of belonging somewhere. Of standing on the ground where his grandfather, and his grandfather's father had stood. That was what had made him who he was today. He couldn't take that away from his child, however much pain it might cause in the short term.

What was he going to tell his dad about Elspeth? he wondered. His father wasn't entitled to know *anything* about his life. Maybe he wouldn't tell him anything. Just show up with a noticeably pregnant woman and let his dad work it out. It wasn't as if he owed him an explanation.

But that wouldn't be fair on Elspeth, he knew. It probably wasn't really fair to take her up there with him at all. If she hadn't suggested it—insisted on it—he wouldn't have thought about doing it. He shouldn't be letting anyone else see into the middle of the conflict between him and his dad. But he was going to—because she had offered and because, selfishly, he wanted her there.

He didn't know what was going on between himself and Elspeth. Other than that they were both keeping a sensible distance from the fireworks that had got them into this situation in the first place. When they had been looking at the apartment the chemistry between them had been so hot that he had been tempted—*so* tempted—to forget all the reasons why they both knew it was a bad idea to be anything other than friends.

And now he had to go and see his father—the perfect reminder of where things led when you made decisions based on what your body wanted, rather than making rational, sensible decisions that protected everybody.

Talking about his father had cured him of that temptation. Or had put it in its proper place at least. He wasn't sure he would ever be cured of wanting her, but the memory of what those sorts of emotions had done to his family was enough to keep his feelings in check. However much he might want Elspeth—and right now he wanted her in every possible way—the only way to keep his family safe and secure and together was to bury those feelings deep.

He dialled his father's number and felt a heavy roiling anxiety as he waited for him to answer.

CHAPTER SEVEN

ELSPETH WATCHED THE landscape change from the window of Fraser's muddy black four-by-four as they drove north. The busy city streets gave way to the suburbs north of Edinburgh, a view of the water as they crossed the new bridge over the Firth of Forth, and then miles of lowland motorway surrounded by fields.

As the motorway gave way to A roads, mountains appeared on the horizon, heavy with snow. The sunlight caught the jewel-bright greens of the grasses and the trees in the fields, popping against the layered taupes and greys of the hills and Munros. Clouds shrouded the higher peaks, and the tops of even the lower hills were covered with snow.

It would be bleak up here in a cold snap, she thought, noting the snow poles either side of the carriageway, just in case the snow hid the road completely.

Elspeth shivered and cranked up the heating, glad that they had taken Fraser's luxury car rather than her old wheelchair-friendly eco-wagon.

Elspeth was growing more and more edgy, she realised, as they racked up the miles between her and Sarah, but at least she knew her mum was there to keep an eye on things. After Elspeth, she knew Sarah's needs better than anyone. And, although they had arranged for some respite cover to help out with the stuff that arthritis made difficult—lifting and transferring Sarah, the physiotherapy that eased the tightness out of her muscles—her mum would be there to supervise.

'There are some blankets behind your seat if the heater's not enough,' Fraser said, spotting her fiddling with the controls and distracting her from her worry for a moment.

She reached behind her and tucked one of the blankets around herself, wondering what this journey would be like with a baby. They'd been on the road for a couple of hours now, and the landscape grew more beautiful, more dramatic, by the mile.

The lush greens of the lowlands had given way to the starker browns and greys of the Cairngorms, broken up by the rich greens of the pine forests. And as the landscape had changed so had Fraser.

In Edinburgh he'd seemed almost cheerful, but Elspeth had been able to see the effort he was having to put in to the façade. There had seemed little point mentioning it, though, when they both understood how complicated his feelings about this trip were. If he wanted to cover his real feelings with false chirpiness, then that was his prerogative. But as they had drawn closer and closer to his childhood home the pretence had fallen away, and now she could see the tension in his features. In the stiff line of his shoulders and his white-knuckled grip on the steering wheel.

'Are you okay?' she asked, not expecting anything more than the 'Fine' that he forced out through gritted teeth.

He wasn't exactly the 'talking about his feelings' type. Especially, she kept reminding herself, as they were only friends. Despite the bump that was growing large enough to make her uncomfortable from time to time.

She rubbed her belly without thinking, and it was only when Fraser said, 'Everything okay in there?' that she realised that he was watching her. Or at least glancing over at her whenever an occasional straight section of road allowed.

'Aside from the dance party we're all fine,' she replied with a smile.

'Dance party?'

'The baby's usually pretty active this time of the evening.'

'Can I feel?'

Elspeth glanced at the twisting road ahead, pretty sure that she didn't want Fraser driving without both hands on the wheel. But before she had a chance to register what he was doing he had pulled over into a gateway leading down a dirt track and was looking at her with earnest longing on his face.

'Can I?'

Elspeth shrugged, trying to pretend that the thought of his hand on her body was something that only concerned her in her role as a mother. Trying to block out the memories of any other time his hand had stroked the soft, naked skin of her belly. This was it. This was who they were to each other now. Co-parents of this life growing—and apparently somersaulting—inside her.

'Sure.' Elspeth heard how steady her voice was and was quietly impressed with her composure.

She didn't exactly feel steady inside. But it didn't help her or Fraser for him to know that. She hitched up her T-shirt—she'd had to give in and buy some maternity tops the week before—and waited for the touch of his hand.

Though the car had warmed up, when Fraser's hand brushed against her skin his fingers were like ice. She yelped and he pulled away, his face a picture of concern.

'Did I hurt you?' he asked.

'Of course not.' Elspeth smiled. 'I'm not that fragile. But your hands are freezing.'

She pulled his hand back and chafed it between her own, rubbing warmth into his fingers.

'Try just here,' she said, placing his hand low on her belly, where the low-cut waistband of her jeans met bare skin. 'It'll still be cold enough to make the baby jump.'

They sat in silence as they waited, their breath starting to steam up the windows. As the minutes went past, and baby kept them waiting, Elspeth pulled the blanket around her again, concealing Fraser's hand beneath. They had both scooted sideways in their seats, to try and bridge the space between them over the car's central console, but after a few minutes Elspeth's back started to ache.

She stretched up, trying to ease out the knot in her spine without dislodging Fraser's hand. She knew that it was always when she took her hand away that the baby would decide to kick up a storm.

'Sure you're okay?' Fraser asked, and this time she was touched rather than amused by his expression.

It was protective, fiercely so, but also tender. Above all, it was intimate. It was a look that told her that they were bound together by this baby, whether they liked it or not. That, as much as they didn't know about each other yet, they were going to be tied together for a lifetime.

'Come here.'

Fraser wound his free arm around her back and pulled her closer to him, turning her slightly so that her back rested against his front. For a moment she stiffened, knowing that being so close to him was a bad idea. It was bad for her self-control, bad for keeping her fantasies at bay. But it felt so right just now, in this minute, as they shared the moment.

She relaxed into him, sliding her hand on top of his where it still rested on her belly. She couldn't feel anything from baby—none of the little flutters or rolls she was slowly getting used to. Instead she could just feel Fraser. The slight scratch of his fingertips against her skin. The caress of his thumb as it started to drift back and forth across her belly. The heat of his breath against her neck, stirring her hair, warming her far more than she should expect from simple body heat.

His arms wrapped tighter around her and his lips tickled the sensitive skin behind her ear as they brushed against her skin. Not a kiss. Not quite—not yet. Without letting herself think too much about it, she let her head drop to one side, giving him more room, more temptation. As his lips finally pressed against her in a hot, moist kiss she felt a jolt low down in her belly, and it was only when Fraser exclaimed behind her that she realised that the baby had finally kicked.

'Oh, my goodness!' Fraser said, a laugh in his voice. 'Was that it? Was that the baby?'

'Well, it wasn't me,' Elspeth said, also laughing, relieved that they had been interrupted before either of them had done something they couldn't take back.

The interruption had chased the heated atmosphere out of the car and replaced it with something less dangerous as their focus centred entirely on the baby.

'Will it do it again?' Fraser asked.

'Probably—give her a minute.'

'Her?' Fraser looked at her with curiosity. 'I thought you weren't finding out.'

'I haven't. It's just habit,' Elspeth explained with a smile and a shrug. 'I have to call her something.'

'It's really real, isn't it?' Fraser said, with something close to wonder in his voice. 'We're really having a baby. *This* baby.'

'We really are,' Elspeth said, resting back in her seat and pulling the blanket tighter. 'Are you okay?' she asked eventually, when Fraser's silence stretched out.

'I am. I just can't quite believe it, you know? You, and the bairn and going home…'

Elspeth reached for his hand, knowing what a concession she'd just got, with Fraser acknowledging his nerves about where they were going.

'I know. I know it's all sudden, and it's all hard. But we're a team.' She squeezed his hand and the baby kicked again, right into Fraser's palm. 'All three of us.'

Fraser smiled and removed his hand, shifting back so he was sitting properly behind the wheel. 'Then I should probably drive us all there and get it over and done with.'

He resumed his grip on the wheel, but the smile that had reached his eyes when he had felt the baby kick was still there, still curling up the corners of his lips too.

That almost-kiss had been nothing, Elspeth told herself. It had just been them sharing a baby milestone, forcing them into the sort of everyday intimacy that expectant couples shared. They had forgotten themselves momentarily, forgotten that the normal rules didn't apply for them. It had made them confuse having feelings for the baby for feelings for each other.

It didn't have to mean anything. It definitely didn't mean that they had to do or say anything. It was best forgotten about.

As the single track road they had been following for a few miles gave way to a gravel driveway Elspeth got her first proper look at the castle. She'd tried to find an image of it online before they had left, but the public highway ended miles from the castle itself, and the satellite pictures had offered up only a grainy bird's eye view.

The car swept around a bend in the driveway, the row of pine trees broke, and Elspeth got her first understanding of what this life was going to mean for her baby.

The ruins of an old castle sat atop a steep

grassy bank in front of a small loch, most of the stones fallen, but a few arches and windows intact. With a nearly full moon reflecting off the water, creating dramatic shadows, Elspeth could only imagine the grandeur of the building in its heyday. And between the car and the ruins sat Castle Ballanross in its second incarnation, with its grey stone, round towers and steeple-like turrets. A burn skirted the farthest corner of the castle, and she wound her window down to hear the gentle burble of water over cobbles.

She tried to imagine a young Fraser here, running around the grounds. It was difficult to see this place as a home. Hard to see it as anything other than a tourist attraction or a relic from the past. She glanced over at Fraser to see how he was taking being back. But his face only showed the same tension that had been present since they'd passed the Cairngorms.

Fraser stopped the car and a door in the tower closest to them opened inwards, silhouetting a figure in the light that spilt from inside. Fraser didn't make any move to open the door, and that was enough for her to know that the man who had opened the door must be his father. She didn't know anything, know any*one* else who could stop Fraser in his tracks like that.

Just as she was wondering whether she would have to say something, Fraser heaved out a sigh and reached for the handle. He paused for a second and looked over at her.

'Look, if this gets ugly, I'm sorry.'

Elspeth took hold of the hand that was still on the steering wheel.

'Don't forget: we're a team. I've got your back.'

Fraser laughed, breaking the tension in the car. 'You make it sound like a duel, or something. I promise it won't come to that.'

Elspeth smiled. 'Good to hear. Now, get your backside out of the car. I'm freezing.'

He laughed again, and Elspeth relaxed just a fraction. Maybe this wouldn't be so bad, after all.

CHAPTER EIGHT

FRASER WALKED TOWARDS the door, his eyes fixed on his father. It had been a decade and a half since he had last seen him, but he could still recognise him just by his silhouette. He felt a spark of annoyance towards himself at that. How much of this man was still a part of him, even after Fraser had tried to pretend for fifteen years that he didn't exist?

Fraser shook his head as he walked closer. How were they meant to do this? He wasn't sure that it was possible to rebuild a relationship that had long-ago burnt out and gone cold. Would his father even want to? He'd had every opportunity over the past fifteen years to get in touch. To try and restart their relationship. And he hadn't tried—not even once.

He thought about the baby Elspeth was carrying, the little flutter of life that he had felt in the car on the way here. That was why he was doing this. Because that child had a place here, on this land, the place where Fraser had always felt anchored. Whole.

Whole.

He couldn't remember when it had started to feel normal to have such a huge part of himself missing. But as he looked around, took in the buildings and landscapes and sounds and smells of his childhood, he realised that he had been living with an enormous part of himself absent for longer than he could remember. And as he looked over to the door and saw his father standing there he was reminded of the reason.

This was his father's fault.

Yes, Fraser was the one who had walked away and refused to look back. But he never would have done that if his father hadn't torn his family apart. Hadn't humiliated his mother by abandoning her for another woman. If he hadn't been blinded by lust and infatuation and mistaken that for love. The sort of love that he and his mother had offered unquestioningly until his father had thrown it back in their faces.

He reached his dad and stuck out a hand in a gesture of greeting. He was the one who had arranged this reunion, and it was going to be on his terms. He would make sure his father understood that.

'Fraser,' his father said, with a waver in his voice.

'Father.'

Fraser noticed that his own voice was deeper than his father's, and that he'd managed to keep it unquestionably solid. He wouldn't give even a hint that he felt anything other than entirely unmoved about this reunion.

This was about the baby. Making sure that his child would have the place in the world it would be born to. That his child wouldn't feel the emptiness Fraser had struggled to fill since he was a teenager. His child belonged here—in this castle, on this land. That was why he was back. The fact that it meant a rapprochement with his dad wasn't relevant to this meeting.

'And will you introduce me to your friend?' his dad asked, his eyeline passing over Fraser's shoulder to where Elspeth was climbing down from the car, her bump hidden in the shadows and folds of her coat.

He hadn't mentioned the baby to his father. In the end he hadn't known how to. He had just told him on the phone that he wanted to come up to the castle and talk.

Would he have guessed? If he had, he would probably be expecting that they were at least in a relationship, if not preparing to get married.

A knot in his stomach reminded him that he had known all along that it wasn't fair to drop Elspeth into this. That he should have explained the situation to his dad before bringing her up here. She was being dropped into the middle of a family drama, and the fact that he hadn't told his dad about the nature of their relationship was only going to make things worse.

He took a deep breath. It was too late to have regrets now. Elspeth was here with him and he couldn't make himself want to change anything about that. He'd take anything to distract himself from the enormity of being back here.

Of going back on his promise to himself that he would never see his father again.

'Father, this is Elspeth,' Fraser said, placing an arm around her waist as she drew near to him.

He knew that it wasn't going to help with the mixed signals, but he wanted her near. Wanted the child within her body near, to remind him why he was doing this. To remind him of his responsibilities to the next generation of his family, the reason why he was here.

'Elspeth, this is Malcolm.'

Elspeth held out a hand and shook Malcolm's with a smile. 'Pleasure to meet you,' she said. 'Thank you for having me in your home.'

'You're very welcome,' he replied, with a curious look towards her middle. 'I'm glad to have you both here.'

Fraser felt anger rising within him. Because his father *did* look pleased. More than pleased. He looked delighted, if a little confused, and Fraser could guess at what he was thinking. He was thinking that this meant a rapprochement, an improvement in relations with his only son. He thought that he was being forgiven.

Well, he could go on thinking that for as long as he wanted. It wasn't going to make it happen. As soon as they were settled inside he would tell his father about the baby and explain that that was the only reason they were here. He would nip any expectations of reconciliation and forgiveness in the bud.

'Well, come in from the cold, both of ye,' Malcolm said after another awkward moment. 'There's a fire in the study—or the kitchen will be warm.'

'The study will be fine,' Fraser said, rejecting instinctively the idea of them all sitting around the range in the kitchen, scene of childhood lunches, hot chocolate and warm bread straight from the oven. The more formal study in the family apartments would be quite sufficient for making introductions and explanations. Then he and Elspeth could get to bed, and at least day one of this trip would be over.

Tomorrow he planned to be out through the door at dawn, looking over Ballanross. Making peace with his long absence and soaking up enough of the air to keep him going until the next time he had to come back.

He moved his hand from around Elspeth's waist, sensing the stiffness and awkwardness in her body. But he couldn't let her go entirely. When he moved his arm away he felt adrift, so he reached for her hand, hoping for an anchor. She laced her fingers between his and squeezed, and he let out a breath of relief that in her he had a friend and an ally.

But that was all he could think of her as. All he should expect from her. If he thought back to that moment that they had shared in the car, a moment that had promised so much more than friendship, he…

He couldn't. It was too confusing. Too distracting. He was grateful for her support in seeing his father for the first time in fifteen years, but he mustn't let himself be distracted by their attraction to one another. There were enough emotions, enough ghosts, flying around this castle without confusing one another by trying to make this relationship something that it could never be.

They followed Malcolm down a chilly corridor—so much colder than Fraser remembered from his childhood. Then, the grand formal rooms had been cold, but the small number of rooms where the family had really lived, where they'd spent their days—carpeted, centrally heated and free of cobwebs—had felt cosy.

In his father's study, a small fire burned in the grate, but even with the flames dancing in front of him Fraser could feel the chill in the room. He tried not to take it as an omen. He should have warned Elspeth to pack extra layers. He wasn't sure that a city girl like her could even conceive of the chill of a Highland castle in winter.

Or maybe he had just gone soft, he thought to himself, shivering again.

'Sorry about the cold,' Malcolm said, adding a couple of logs to the fire. 'I've had it burning in here all day, but this place takes weeks to warm up if it gets cold. Well, you remember…' he said, trying to meet Fraser's eyes.

No, Fraser thought. *You don't get to do that. You don't get to call on our shared history and pretend that nothing has happened. You don't get to dip into my past and bring it into the present at will.*

It was only as his anger subsided that he

started to process his father's words. Weeks to warm up? Why wasn't the central heating on? And if that wasn't enough to keep the place warm why wasn't he burning a fire in here every day?

He looked around the study and found it much as he remembered it from fifteen years ago. His father's old desk was laden with papers, and the same antique armchairs stood by the fire.

But the upholstery was worn through, showing the stuffing underneath. He didn't know what had happened in the intervening years, but he remembered the furniture in here gleaming, proudly withstanding the decay that had claimed most pieces of that vintage. But now there was dust everywhere, knocks and rings showing on the wood and the smell of damp in the air. It was clear that standards had slipped considerably.

He shook his head, resisting the urge to interfere in the upkeep of the estate. It wasn't his responsibility. Not anymore. Not yet.

When they were all seated by the fire his father looked at them both expectantly, and at last Fraser dropped Elspeth's hand. It was hardly worth the gesture; his father would have jumped to conclusions already. And he missed the warmth of her. The reassurance. The feeling that they were in this as a team. But it was done now.

'Father, my friend Elspeth and I are expecting a baby.' He emphasised *'friend'*, hoping that it would get rid of the need for further explanations.

His father's smile beamed from every feature, travelling from his mouth to his eyes, and taking in every line and crag of his skin in between.

'Well, that's wonderful news…'

Questions remained unspoken but hung in the room around him. *And...? And we're getting married... And we're an item...*

And it was none of his business, Fraser thought. He had long ago given up the right to ask those sorts of questions. They were here for the baby—not because he owed his father anything.

'I'd like Ballanross to be a part of the baby's life from the start. That's why we're here.'

That was what was important here. His child's land and legacy. His family's responsibility to the people who relied on the estate for their livelihoods. The privileges and responsibilities that his son or daughter would one day inherit.

'Well, I'm very pleased to see you,' Malcolm said, not seeming the least bit put out that Fraser had just told him that he hadn't come here to see *him*. 'And to hear your news. That's wonderful. When is the baby due?'

Malcolm's placatory words made Fraser even more angry. How could he act as if nothing was wrong? As if he *hadn't* destroyed their family and kept Fraser away from his home for fifteen years? As if Fraser *hadn't* spent the whole of his adult life hating him?

Before he realised what he was doing he had pushed to his feet and balled his hands into fists to stop them doing something that he would regret. The rage that he had bottled up for fifteen years was making a break for it, and he couldn't let that happen. He couldn't lose control of his emotions like that. He knew better. Knew better than his father ever had.

He took one more look at Malcolm and felt such anger that he knew he had to walk away. He strode from the room, his feet marching ahead under their own volition, carrying him towards his childhood bedroom.

As he pushed open the door he realised that nothing had been changed in here since the day he had left. The few books he'd forgotten to pack had been tidied from the floor. The bed had been stripped. But there were still posters on the wall, a few old toys on the shelves. He dropped down onto the bed, feeling like the angry teenager he had been the last time he was in this room.

Elspeth took a deep breath before knocking on the door. Malcolm had directed her to Fraser's old bedroom—his best guess as to where he might have gone when he had stormed off. She had known from the start that this visit was going to be difficult for them all—Fraser most of all. But she hadn't expected it to be quite so dramatic quite so early on.

Fraser hadn't been kidding when he'd said that things were bad between him and his dad.

For a minute she'd wondered whether they'd made a big mistake, coming all the way up here just to reignite a family feud. But then the baby had given her a sharp kick—a timely reminder that she didn't want any bad feeling in this family, *her* family now. She wanted her baby born into love and peace and harmony, however hippy that might sound. And, while it might be a bit optimistic hoping that Fraser and his father would be all warm hugs and bonhomie by the end of the weekend, it didn't seem unreasonable to think that they might at least be civil to one another.

She knocked and turned the handle, and found Fraser sitting on an antique panelled bed hung with heavy navy and gold drapes, looking not a little lost.

He stood as she walked in and rubbed the back of his neck. 'How did you find me?'

'Your dad thought you might be up here.'

Elspeth's instinct was to reach out to him, offer comfort. Pull him into her arms. But she knew that if she did that there would be much more than comfort between them. They had proved that in the car on the way up here.

Any physical contact between them was a bad idea. They couldn't be trusted to keep things innocent.

'Your dad gave me directions,' she carried on, trying to shake the memories of what had happened earlier. 'Should have drawn me a map. I'll never find my way back.'

Fraser gave a smile, more in recognition of her attempt to lighten the mood than at her humour.

'I shouldn't have walked out,' Fraser said.

Not quite an apology, she noticed. In the circumstances, she could understand, but that didn't mean she was going to let him get away with it.

'And you shouldn't have left me sitting there. I said I'd be your wingman, not your cleanup crew.'

Another smile, less forced this time.

'I know. You're a hero. I shouldn't have walked out like that.'

Elspeth smiled. Knowing that he'd been an idiot didn't get him off the hook either. She dropped to sit on his bed, stretching out her back and taking in her surroundings. The posters on the wall, the figures on the shelves.

'Is this just how you left it?' she asked, to break the silence.

'Aye.' Fraser nodded. 'It's a little tidier now. But this was me at fifteen.'

'Does it feel strange?' Elspeth asked, realising what an intimate thing it was, to walk into a room and see someone's childhood. 'To come back and find it like this?'

Fraser shrugged. 'I don't know. I assume you still have your childhood room, if you're living with your mum. Is that weird?'

'Yes, honestly, it is sometimes.'

She might as well tell the truth. Living with her mum when she was in her thirties was never going to be ideal. But she didn't have the luxury of another choice. Her mum and Sarah needed her to be there.

'But my room isn't a time capsule,' she went on, after sitting quietly for a few moments. 'Your dad could have changed things in here. Taken down the posters. Even if you were going to come back he had to know that you wouldn't need a teenager's bedroom any more.'

Fraser's face hardened into an expression that came out whenever they talked about his father. 'Probably he just didn't care. I doubt he's been in here since I left.'

'Looks pretty clean and tidy in here for a room that's not been touched for fifteen years.'

Fraser didn't have an answer for that. All right, she knew that generally a castle came with an army of staff to look after it, but there was no denying that this room was well-kept. Better kept, in fact, than the room they had been in earlier.

It looked as if she had given Fraser something to think about, because he had sat back on the bed and rested forward on his elbows, staring pensively at the floor.

Did he really think that? Elspeth wondered. That his father didn't care about him? Because it had been clear to her from the moment she had seen Malcolm waiting in the doorway of the tower, nervous anticipation obvious in his posture, that Malcolm cared very deeply about his son. But if Fraser really thought that his father didn't love him, what had that done to him over the years? To the way he saw himself? To his relationships? No wonder he had been scared when she had told him about the baby. If he hadn't ever been able to count on this most important bond, no wonder he had never made another.

Not that it mattered to *her*, she reminded herself. Fraser's commitment issues weren't her problem and they weren't why she wasn't interested in a relationship with him. There was way more than that standing between them and a happy-ever-after. It was good to have the reminder, though. That it wasn't just her who didn't want this.

Even if Sarah was suddenly cured and Elspeth's responsibilities magically melted away and her time and emotional energy and love weren't pulling her in three different directions, Fraser was in no position to be in a relationship.

All they had to concentrate on was being the best parents they could be to this baby. And as far as she could see, Fraser wasn't going to be able to do that until he'd fully come to terms with the breakdown of his relationship with his father. And perhaps tried to make a new relationship with him.

Elspeth reached for Fraser's hand, remembering how much she'd liked the way he'd held it earlier. She'd liked the way it had felt to be anchored to him. Liked the way it had felt, knowing that he'd come to her for support.

She was his family now, she realised, and felt the reality of their situation sinking in yet another level. She was the mother of his child, and that meant they shared a bond that would last for ever. She couldn't escape from it, even if she wanted to.

She couldn't think how she'd find the capacity to care for someone else, and suddenly wondered what she was doing here, in the Highlands, digging herself deeper into family issues that had been impossible to fix long before *she* had had anything to do with Fraser.

She gasped in a short breath as the baby kicked her ribs and she rubbed against them absent-mindedly.

'Can I feel?' Fraser asked.

She remembered the atmosphere between them in the car. How a simple touch had escalated so quickly into something that she had been so sure neither one of them would want—until they hadn't been able to help themselves. But she *wanted* him to touch her. This was his child—they had agreed to parent together and this was a part of that. It was something that they should share.

She shrugged her shoulders, faking a nonchalance that she absolutely did not feel, and then held dead still, resisting any reaction to the feel of Fraser's touch on her skin. She held her breath for a few seconds, willing the baby to kick quickly. For once the baby co-operated and gave its father a quick tap on the hand, cueing a snort of laughter from Fraser.

'I can't get over how amazing that feels,' he said with another laugh, breaking the tension in the room. 'How do you concentrate on anything when you have a whole person in there, trying to get your attention?'

Elspeth smiled. 'She doesn't make it easy. But it started gradually and I guess I've got used to it.'

'I can't imagine *ever* getting used to it.'

The wonder in Fraser's voice was intoxicating, and it caught them up for another few minutes, as they quietly waited for the baby to kick again. But then real life started to creep back in, and Elspeth couldn't help but point out the obvious.

'Well, she's not going to be in there for ever.'

Fraser withdrew his hand and coughed awkwardly. 'I guess not. I can't believe it's going so quickly. A few more months and everything's going to change.'

She made an effort to smile, but couldn't help feeling a twinge of anxiety. Not everything was going to change. Much of her life would stay the same. Her work. Her career. Her caring responsibilities. They weren't all going to fade away just because she had this enormous new challenge coming. They were all going to be just as demanding as ever.

Something of what she was thinking must have shown on her face, because Fraser took her hand back into his and gave it a squeeze.

'It's all right to be scared. But we're in this together.'

Sure they were. The baby part of it. But he

wasn't the one who was going to have to fight to get his career back on track post-maternity leave. He wasn't the one who was going to have to call around for emergency cover when Sarah was sick. He wasn't going to be taking on the challenges that she already dealt with every day.

'Stop it,' he said gently. 'Whatever spiral you're heading down, I promise you we are going to make this work. Have you called home since we got here?' he asked, showing more insight than she'd realised he had.

'They're fine,' she said, reflexively tapping her phone through the fabric of her pocket, reminding herself that they could get hold of her if they needed to. 'I'm just not used to being away from home for more than a night.'

He pulled her down beside him on the bed as they both looked up to the ancient beams of the ceiling.

'I was surprised when you agreed to stay a few days,' Fraser admitted.

'I was being realistic about how much time you and your father might need,' Elspeth replied. 'And when you asked… I don't know. Objectively, three nights away didn't seem like that long. But now that we're here… I feel so far away. I feel helpless.'

Fraser squeezed her hand in support. 'But you know that your sister is safe. That your mum has the help she needs from the agency care assistants.'

'I know all that. I do. But… It's just hard to turn off the part of my brain that feels it should be doing something.'

'You *are* doing something,' Fraser said, letting go of her hand and rubbing the swell of her belly. 'You're growing this wee bairn, for a start.'

Elspeth let out something between a moan and a sigh at the feel of his touch on her tight skin. But being surrounded by Fraser's childhood things, both gazing upwards, not making eye contact, made the atmosphere quietly intimate rather than sexy.

'Mmm… And that's not getting any easier,' she admitted.

His palm traced circles over her skin, over their baby. 'How are you feeling?'

She let out a sigh. 'Tired, if I'm honest. And clumsy. And achy.'

She let out a squeak of protest as Fraser dropped her hand and pushed at her hip, rolling her on to her side with her back to him. His hands rested on her, applying gentle pressure, teasing knots from her neck and her shoulders, travelling down the length of her spine until they pressed hard into the small of her back.

'You should have said something,' Fraser said, his voice soft and close to her ear.

'I can't—'

'It's just a massage,' Fraser said, and she could hear the smile on his lips. 'This is something friends do for each other, right?'

She really wasn't sure about that. She'd never had a friend touch her like this before. Never felt so electric with a friend's hands stroking her. But then, she'd never had a baby with a friend either. She wasn't sure there was a rulebook for this sort of friendship. Certainly no one had given her one.

'Is it helping?'

She let out another long sigh, losing the ability to articulate.

Fraser laughed behind her, a warm little burst of breath on her neck. 'I'll take that as a yes,' he said, working his thumbs beside her spine until her body felt like jelly.

Then he lay back, and she followed, until they were both staring up at the ceiling once more.

'You know,' Fraser said, speaking softly, 'I think we make a good team.'

CHAPTER NINE

FRASER HAD LEFT her loose-limbed and relaxed at the door of an extravagantly decorated guest room with a kiss on the cheek and a pile of blankets spread on the feather eiderdown that topped the four-poster bed.

When she woke, pale sunlight was trying to make its way through the dust and condensation on the windows. She lifted her head from the pillows and goosebumps immediately broke out on her shoulders and arms. It was chilly in here. Forget that—it was downright freezing.

She pulled one of the blankets from the bed and wrapped it around her shoulders while she went and wrestled with the valve of the enormous and ancient radiator over by the windows.

She used the corner of the blanket to rub a clear patch in a pane of the glass and had her first proper glimpse of Ballanross in the daylight. The driveway that they had crunched across last night curved dramatically through the landscape, past the ruins of the old castle, which sat majestically on the top of the hillside. Snow was visible on the tops of the mountains to the west, and the loch was fishpond-calm behind the old castle. The pale sun was low in the sky to the east, trying valiantly to warm the picturesque Scottish scene—without much luck.

A door slammed somewhere below and Fraser strode purposefully out of the door, wrapped up in a heavy winter jacket and hiking boots, and peered up at the tallest tower. So much for being a team, Elspeth thought. He was leaving her alone with his father—*again*. She wasn't sure how he was meant to get anywhere with fixing this relationship if he was going to be out through the door at first light.

She checked the time on her phone—it was past nine already. She held on to the hope that Fraser and Malcolm had had a heart-to-heart over breakfast, but knew that it was unlikely.

Crossing over to her suitcase, she hunted out

warm layers and thick hiking socks, and even considered for a moment going straight out to catch Fraser before he left. But then a jab in the ribs and a rumble in her stomach reminded her that she wasn't alone, and that the baby was demanding breakfast even if Elspeth thought there were more important things to be doing.

Trying to retrace her steps from the night before, she took a wrong turn and found herself in a grand hall adorned with suits of armour criss-crossed with cobwebs and an armoury's worth of weapons mounted on the wall. She spun in a slow circle, looking up, taking in the faded splendour of the castle, trying to imagine a childhood spent running through these hallways, amidst these riches, this history.

Would their child feel like the castle and the land was a part of them, as Fraser so obviously did? Or would she always feel the outsider? Feel the echo of the estrangement between Fraser and his father? Feel the city child, out of place in the country, like Elspeth did right now?

She turned sharply at the sound of footsteps behind her, and smiled when she saw Malcolm walking towards her, carrying a cup of coffee that was steaming heavily in the chill of the room.

'Ah, good morning,' he said with a smile. 'I was wondering if I should bring you a cup, but then I saw ye come through this way and thought you might need directions. Let's go on back to the kitchen and I'll put the kettle on.'

She followed him through a warren of hallways until they reached the kitchen. A copper *batterie de cuisine* hung on the wall, covered with a layer of the dust she had seen everywhere else, and Malcolm went to fill the plastic kettle, yellowed slightly with age, that sat on a worktop.

'Will you have coffee or tea?' Malcolm asked as he fussed around finding a mug and some milk. 'You'll have to excuse the place. The housekeeper is only here three days a week, and there's really too much for her to manage. I do my best, but with a place this size you're never going to win.'

'I can imagine,' Elspeth said, and tried to hide the many, many questions she had about this. A housekeeper only three days a week?

No wonder the place was looking tired. From what little Fraser had told her about his childhood here she had been expecting to find at least a few members of full-time staff, and more out in the grounds.

Not that she didn't think Malcolm could take care of himself, but a building like this needed specialist care. It was more than one person—*any* one person—could manage by themselves.

She made small talk as she drank her tea and ate a couple of slices of toast, and then took a deep breath, unsure what reaction she would get to her next question.

'Did you see Fraser this morning?'

'Mmmph…'

The sadness in the older man's expression tugged at her sympathy, and she knew that she had guessed right—Fraser had been out through the door without a word for his father this morning.

'Well, Fraser's not one for being kept still for long. He said something about taking a look at the north tower. Had a quick look outside and then came in and headed up the staircase.'

'I think I'll try and find him,' Elspeth said.

'Are you sure?'

'If you don't mind, of course,' she added, not wanting to be rude. 'I'll look for him inside first. And if he's not here I'll take a quick look outdoors.'

And hopefully she'd catch up with him and talk some sense into him, she added in her head. Remind him that they'd driven all the way up here so that Fraser could actually *talk* to his father, rather than put as much distance between them as possible at the earliest opportunity.

'Aye, well, if you can find him...' Malcolm added. 'But he could have taken one of the quad bikes. And—no offence, lass—I'm not letting you take one of those in your condition.'

Elspeth smiled, touched at his concern for her, even though she would have accused anyone other than her child's grandfather of blatant sexism.

'In any case I won't go far,' she promised, 'indoors or out. And if I don't bump into him, then I'll come back. Don't worry, I won't be hiking up a mountain alone.'

Malcolm nodded. 'I'll walk with you inside,

if you like. I usually just keep to the family rooms. It'll be good for me to see the place through new eyes. And it'd be…good to walk with Fraser a while, if we find him.'

'Thank you,' Elspeth said, clocking his wistful expression, hearing the pain and longing in his voice. His love for his son was so palpable she couldn't believe that Fraser was refusing to see it. In her line of work she saw a lot of family politics. People who—under the great strain that ill-health put on families—turned on the ones they loved.

Occasionally she saw those families find a way back together. But she'd also seen estrangements that had festered until it was too late. She had seen loneliness that had become pathological, contributing to the misery of patients nearing the end of their lives. She wouldn't allow that to happen here. She wouldn't allow Fraser—that pig-headed man—to leave this place until he'd at least had a proper conversation with his father.

And she didn't care if that made her meddling and interfering. This was *her* family now, and that gave her every right to be involved.

She pulled on the fleece that she'd intended to wear outside, not realising that she would need it in the castle too. And as she left the kitchen with Malcolm she could feel a draught straight down the corridor. She stuffed her hands deep into her pockets, wondering whether it would be rude to put on her gloves and scarf too.

The further they walked around the castle, the clearer it became that it was falling into serious disrepair. The wind whistled through broken window panes, and there was a dampness in the air that spoke of long-set neglect.

Elspeth followed Malcolm down a long gallery that seemed to take them away from the inhabited part of the castle—away from carpets and radiators and home comforts, even the chilly and draughty kind. These rooms were imposing and echoing—lined with historical relics collecting dust. Where Malcolm's apartment was comfily shabby, these rooms were a testament to a grand way of living that had long since ceased to be practical.

They found Fraser in a small room high up in the north tower, inspecting another broken window pane—or was he looking out over the estate?

He turned as they crossed the threshold into the room. His expression shifted through surprise to anger in the split second it took for him to register Malcolm behind her.

'What are you doing up here?' he asked, the question clearly directed more at his father than at her.

'I wanted to see some more of the castle,' Elspeth said, feeling the tension in the room and wondering whether she had made a huge mistake. 'Malcolm offered to show me. We thought we might catch up with you.'

But she could see that he wasn't really listening to her answer. His eyes hadn't left his father when she'd spoken, and anger was clear in every line of his face.

'Look at the state of this place,' Fraser said, gesturing towards the window, knowing that he was letting his anger show.

How had his father let it come to this? It was hard to believe how badly the place had slipped into disrepair and decay in the years that Fraser had been gone.

'What's happened to it?' he asked, though he didn't really need to. His father had neglected it. He hadn't cared enough about it to take care of it.

His father shifted his feet, and Fraser felt sorry for him for a moment—before he remembered that he was angry with him.

'It takes a lot to keep this place running, Fraser. You know that.'

'Aye. I do,' Fraser replied. 'And I'd be ashamed of myself if the estates *I* managed looked like this.'

From behind his father, he saw Elspeth make a move towards him. For a split second Fraser could taste acid in his mouth as he imagined her walking across the floor. He could almost see the wood breaking apart beneath her feet, could see her falling through to the room below.

He moved faster than he'd known he could, and stopped her with a hand on her arm. 'Don't,' he said, aware that his voice was still tainted with anger, that he was speaking too harshly to her. 'The water has been coming in through the window and the roof. It's rotted the floorboards. It's not safe for you to be in here.'

The thought that something might have happened to her if she'd come up here before he'd pulled back the rug and seen the damage to the floor focussed his anger to a white-hot rage. If she had got hurt it would have been Malcolm's fault. Because of his neglect of this beautiful castle. Of the place where his family should be flourishing if he hadn't thrown it all away over a midlife lust for someone new and desirable.

The castle hadn't looked like this all those nights Fraser had dreamed of it. There had been no broken windows. No rotting joists. He dreaded to think what else he was going to find. How much time and money it was going to take to put it right.

It wasn't his responsibility yet, he tried to tell himself.

Except it was.

If he wanted to come home here one day. If he wanted to raise a family here, he couldn't just leave it to rot away. He had a responsibility to this place. And Ballanross clearly needed him.

He threw another angry look at his father. 'I can't believe you've let this happen.'

'Son, I don't want to argue with you.'

Son? Fraser crossed his arms. Malcolm had lost the right to use that word a long time ago.

'I'm not arguing,' Fraser pointed out. 'I'm asking a very simple question about why vital repairs haven't been done. I'm asking whether you even had a plan to stop this tower rotting straight through to the bare earth. When would you have stepped in? When would you have done something?'

'I had a plan. I have a plan for all the repairs. But they can't all be done at once.'

At once? Fraser thought. He hadn't seen a single thing that his father had done for this place. No doubt once the new wife had moved in there hadn't been time for thinking about floorboards.

His father had chosen his love-life over his responsibilities time and time again. It was clear that his stepmother hadn't cared for this place. He knew that she'd only lived here for two years, but there wasn't a single sign of her. His father had ruined their family for a relationship so insubstantial that it had already disappeared without a trace.

'You haven't done *anything*,' Fraser said. 'It has to start somewhere.'

'Right, lad. And who's going to pay for it?'

Fraser scrubbed his hands through his hair, either side of his head, trying to keep his temper in check. Trying not to lose it with his old man in front of Elspeth. But his father was testing every ounce of his reserve.

'Are you telling me there's no money?' He forced the words out through gritted teeth, the effort of not shouting them making them come out short and clipped. 'What's happened to it?'

Malcolm threw his hands up, but the helplessness of the gesture did nothing to calm Fraser.

'I'm telling you it's impossible to keep up,' Malcolm said. 'I've tried. I *am* trying. But this place soaks up every penny and then comes back asking for more.'

'We have an entire estate to support us.

What's happening to all the rents? What about the investments?'

The money that Fraser had inherited and invested had been doing so well for so long he couldn't believe that the estate that had generated the capital in the first place could be struggling. If he'd known....

What would he have done differently? Forgiven his father and come home?

'I'm doing everything I can, Fraser,' Malcolm said. 'Isn't that enough?'

Fraser gestured towards the rotting floorboards. 'Apparently not.'

'Well, I'd love to hear your suggestions—because I've been doing this on my own for the past fifteen years and I'm out of ideas.'

How dared he throw that at him? Fraser thought. Make it *his* fault because he wasn't here? He'd wanted to be here. He'd wanted his father to choose *him*. But Malcolm hadn't. He had chosen some fickle attachment to a woman who hadn't stuck around.

It had been bad enough when Fraser had thought that it was only feelings that had got hurt. If he'd known that his father was going to sacrifice Ballanross on the altar of his doomed second marriage too, perhaps he'd have been back here years ago, giving him a piece of his mind. Making sure his children's legacy was protected.

Of *course* Fraser had suggestions. He had a whole list of them that he had started as they'd driven up here through the woodland and he'd started to get a sense that the place had been allowed to fall into the sort of state that he would never permit on an estate *he* was managing.

He hadn't seen the accounts, but he'd known even before his father had said anything that they would be as much of a mess as the castle was.

Could he fix it? A twinge of something like guilt pulled at his belly. This would never have happened if he had been here to take care of it. Instead there was an estate three hours' drive from here that was flourishing while his own home was rotting away.

But he would never have had to leave if his

father hadn't chosen his new wife over him. This wasn't his fault. His father had been the adult at the time. This was all on *him*.

He remembered that Elspeth was standing beside him and turned to her.

'Let's go.'

He took her hand, vaguely aware that he was making a bad habit of doing that, and then snatched it back. His father's lust, kept unchecked, had led them here. He wasn't going to perpetuate the problem by making things complicated with Elspeth. Here was a reminder, as if he needed it, that indulging the intense desire he had for her wasn't going to get them anywhere. His father had gone down that path—and look where it had got them.

But Elspeth pulled his hand back, stopping him from storming down the staircase.

'Stop, Fraser. If you're running away from this you're not dragging me with you.'

'Leave it, Elspeth,' he said, still angry. 'You don't need to be involved in this.'

But she tugged at his arm, enough to stop him storming out. 'I do need to be involved. Last time I checked, you two hadn't made such a good job of working this out without me. Now, are we going to talk about this like adults?'

'I'm done talking,' Fraser said, turning for the door again.

'Well, I'm not,' Elspeth declared behind him. 'Malcolm, where's the best place for us to look at everything? The accounts and stuff? I'll help if I can.'

'Well…' Malcolm hesitated. 'If you want I can meet you in my study,' he said, his voice wavering a little. 'But I'm not sure what there is to be done.'

'I don't know how much help I'll be,' Elspeth replied, sounding more unperturbed. 'But I'm willing to try.'

Fraser met Elspeth's eyes and stared, waiting for her to read his silent message: *Keep out of this. I don't need you to interfere. I've got this under control.* But she stared back at him, steadfast, and he knew that she wasn't going to back down.

Fine. He should go through the accounts anyway. His father had been ignoring the problem for long enough—Fraser wasn't going to contribute to his neglect.

'Fine,' Fraser said aloud. 'I'll see you in there.'

He walked back up to the guest room where he had stayed last night and grabbed his laptop. He wasn't sure that he'd need it, but he needed the breather. Needed to be away from Elspeth and his father and let his anger subside.

He had been close to completely losing his temper, and he knew that giving in to those extreme emotions was going to get him nowhere. Since he had left the castle and his childhood behind he'd learnt that he had to keep his feelings in check. Not let them get the better of him. It was impossible to make good decisions based on emotion.

He stood at the window of his room, looking out at the ruins of the old castle, the stones warming in the winter sun, the loch a shimmering silver-gold behind, breathing deep until he felt the muscles of his shoulders relaxing.

He had spent hours up there as a kid. Exploring the old building, trying to imagine the lives of the people who had lived there.

When he was calm again, and could think of the conversation that he had to go and have without clenching his fists, he turned away from the window and headed for the door.

CHAPTER TEN

WHEN FRASER REACHED the study, Elspeth was peering over Malcolm's shoulder at an ancient computer. Thankfully it wasn't the monster of a desktop that he remembered helping his father use before he had left home, but he could tell just by looking at it that it was a good five years past needing replacing. And then there were the papers, stacked on the desk, on the bookshelf, on the floor in front of the leather wingback chair positioned by a cold fireplace.

They must not have heard him over the roar of the old computer's fan, desperately trying to keep the machine from overheating and blowing up. So he leaned against the door frame and watched them for a moment.

Would this ever have been what he wanted? The woman carrying his child getting to know his father? If he hadn't left this place… If his father had never met someone else… If his childhood and everything that had followed hadn't been marked by the choice that his father had made. Would Malcolm still be the man that he remembered before that day? Would his father be a different person? Would he, Fraser, be changed?

He shook his head. There was no point thinking like that. Those things couldn't be undone. They could never go back there.

They had to go forward. They had to try and make a new relationship. It could never be what it was. But he had missed his father. He could admit to himself now that every time he had thought about his home over the years, every time he had felt that emptiness inside him that he thought could be filled by coming home, he had been missing his dad.

But building something new would mean letting go of what had gone before. It would mean forgiveness. And suddenly Fraser knew that he wasn't ready. He couldn't forgive his father… yet. But, seeing him talking with Elspeth, it made him want to. Perhaps one day they could have a relationship again.

He took another step into the room and Elspeth and Malcolm must have heard him, because they both turned to look at him.

'Well, I'm glad you're here,' Elspeth said. 'I'll take brain surgery over *this*. And I say that as someone who has actually performed brain surgery.'

'I'm suitably impressed,' Fraser said with a smile, somewhat relieved to find that it was something he could still do. 'Let me have a look.'

He pushed another chair up to the desk and pulled the laptop towards him. 'Right, then, tell me what I'm looking at.'

His father scrolled through a few tabs and open programs. 'Well, there's the bank accounts, and the investment accounts. Here's my cash flow spreadsheet.'

'Who's the accountant? Still Taylor?'

'No, I had to let him go a few years back. I've been taking care of things myself.'

Fraser gave him a look out of the corner of his eye but resisted saying anything. If he and his father were going to rebuild their relationship one day he was going to have to stop taking cheap shots every time the opportunity presented itself.

He clicked through the windows that Malcolm had left open on the computer and was vaguely aware of the silence that was falling around the three of them as he scrolled through page after page of financial records, trying to resist coming to the conclusion that was becoming harder and harder to escape.

Ballanross was broke. Flat broke. Falling-down broke. His father hadn't been exaggerating. There simply wasn't any money. From what he could work out, it was all gone. Investments had been cashed in for repairs and debts, but with them had gone their income and so the cycle had begun. The situation had gone from bad to worse, and then to worse still, until now there was nothing left, and the mother of his child was walking over a rotting floor four storeys up.

He rubbed his hands through his hair, hoping for the figures to change in front of his eyes, to persuade him that circumstances weren't as bad as he was reading.

'Dad… This is…this is bad.'

'Mmmph.'

The hint of a smile in that one simple syllable made Fraser realise that he'd used the word 'Dad' for the first time since he'd been back. It had fallen from his lips without him thinking.

It was a start.

'What else do I need to know?' Fraser asked, trying to keep his mind on the numbers. On something that he could make sense of.

He was already coming up with ideas to increase their income. How they could use the incredible natural resources of Ballanross to attract visitors and businesses to the area. To halt the decay of the castle until they had the money they needed to make real improvements. He could see it in his mind. He could see the rooms gleaming as they did in his memory. He could see the woodlands properly managed and flourishing. He could see his child running through the halls as if they were a playground, like in his earliest memories.

'You know what? Never mind,' he said. 'We need to go back to basics. Let's look at outgoings first. Where's that bank statement?'

His father pulled it up on the computer and

Fraser went through it again, more slowly this time. He asked questions occasionally, when it wasn't clear what an expense was, and made a few notes on the spreadsheet.

Until he got to a name he recognised and his blood ran cold.

'What is this?' Fraser asked. There was a metallic taste in his mouth, and he hoped that his father wasn't about to say what he was expecting.

His father hesitated for long enough for Fraser to know that he was right, even before he said, 'It's nothing important, Fraser. It's Louise, my…wife. My ex-wife. We're still friends, you see, and she needed to borrow some money for a few weeks. I said I'd loan it to her.'

Fraser could feel the blood rushing to his face as his hands tightened into fists. He fought the reaction down, trying to keep his emotions under control. 'You're lending money to the woman you chose over me while our home is falling down around you? What's *wrong* with you?'

'Ach, Fraser, it's not like that. It's a small loan. If you let me explain…'

Explain? What could he possibly say that would explain this? He didn't want to know that his father was still in touch with his ex-wife. He didn't want to see her name or be reminded that she existed. His father had sacrificed everything for her, for a marriage that had lasted only two years. A flash-in-the-pan relationship that had cost Fraser his family as he knew it.

To know that his dad was still in touch with her, when he himself hadn't spoken to him for so long... He didn't know why that hurt so badly, given that he was the one who had walked away.

He rose to his feet, thinking that perhaps movement would help. That he would be able to walk off this restlessness, settle his heartbeat and find some calm. But instead, as he thought more about how his father had chosen *her*, that other woman, he could feel himself growing more and more angry. Emotions that had been long buried were forcing their way out, pushing him closer and closer to losing control. Tension ripped up through his core, stiffening his shoulders, moving back down to his arms and his fists, and he knew that he was closer than he had ever been to losing control of his feelings.

He headed for the door. Needing to be outside. Needing to escape that toxic atmosphere and get himself back in control. He charged out of the front door out into the grounds and strode across the gravel without a thought to the cold or to the direction he was walking.

Elspeth took the hat, scarf and mittens that Malcolm had pulled for her out of the cupboard by the door and thanked the Scottish weather gods for the weak sun and clear sky. She waved goodbye to Malcolm and headed out of the door and away from the sun, taking the bridge over the burn, and walking down the gravel path that led to the castle ruins and the loch, her shadow stretching far ahead of her. The sun caught on the face of the old stones, which seemed to glow a warm, creamy grey in the soft light.

She couldn't see Fraser yet, but much of the ruins was hidden in shadow, so she walked on.

The look on his face when he had argued

with his father… It had been like a window into the deepest depths of his hurt. As if every doubt and fear that he had held over the whole of his life had re-emerged at once. She had seen the anger crash over him like a wave, and then seen the fear in his face as a response.

He had not walked out of that room because of the anger. He had been afraid. Of what, though? Of what he might say to his father? Of what he might hear? Or was he simply afraid of the feeling itself, overwhelmed by an emotion he wasn't equipped to deal with?

Perhaps she would learn something more about him up here, seeing the place he sought out when he needed to be grounded. Even if he wasn't there she needed to see it, now that Malcolm had told her it meant so much to Fraser. She wanted to know him. To understand him. Because he was the father of her child, she told herself.

But the thought rang false. Like when she glanced at an X-ray and knew there was something wrong before she'd had time to work out what it was.

Her feelings for Fraser had nothing to do with the baby.

She tried to unpick that sensation—the unease of having a thought, a feeling, lurking in her subconscious, just out of reach. If the way she felt about Fraser had nothing to do with him being the father of her child… Then it was *him*.

As soon as she articulated the thought to herself she knew that it was true.

From the first time that she had seen Fraser at Janet's wedding she had wanted him. That hadn't stopped just because of the circumstances that they now found themselves in. She couldn't stop responding to him, remembering the way that she had responded to his body, just because she knew that a relationship with him would never work. She had feelings for him. She admitted it at last.

But that didn't mean she was going to act on those feelings. It didn't mean she was suddenly released from her responsibilities and free to be with him. She'd already proved that she couldn't be in a relationship. Alex had made her choose where her priorities lay, and she had chosen her family. There was no reason the universe would suddenly bend its rules just because she was attracted to Fraser.

The path she was following twisted through a small copse of trees and Elspeth shivered, pulling the hat lower over her ears and the scarf tighter around her neck. When she emerged into the sunshine again she could see a figure up by the ruins, walking slowly along one of the fallen walls, jumping from stone to stone where the grass had grown in—nature reclaiming the site for its own.

She would have known it was Fraser even if Malcolm hadn't told her he would probably be there. She wondered when she had committed it to memory—the shape of his body, the way he moved, how he carried himself.

Had it been that night, when for hours he had been the silhouette between her and the soft glow of a lamp in the corner? When she had traced the contours of his body with her hands and grasped them with her limbs, imprinting the shape of him on her, the feel of his skin, until she knew just where to touch, how to move to elicit a moan or a groan.

She could bring to mind in a fraction of a second the softness of his hair against her breasts, the roughness of his hands as they skimmed down her arms, making her shiver with anticipation. But as she put one foot in front of the other, bringing her closer and closer to where he sat on a collapsed heap of masonry, she knew that she had to concentrate on the reason they had come up to Ballanross rather than on her own feelings.

Fraser had been so angry back in Malcolm's study that she had been half expecting to find him pummelling something with his fists. But it looked as if he had walked off the worst of his mood. She knew that she should talk to him about what had just happened, but she didn't even know where to start. It didn't matter how much she wanted her baby born into a loving, harmonious family—she didn't know how to fix this, how to make them a family. She didn't know how to stop thinking about their night together. She didn't know how she could live with Fraser in her life without thinking of what might have been between them. Without wondering what it would feel like to be touched by him, kissed by him again.

With her eyes fixed on Fraser, she lost sight of her footing, and before she realised what was happening she had caught her toes on a piece of stone hidden among the grass and toppled forward. She let out a squeak of alarm but managed to right herself with nothing but her pride a little dented. She could only hope that Fraser hadn't seen her. She wasn't exactly sure what she was going to say to him, but this wasn't exactly the entrance that she wanted to make.

She brushed imaginary dirt from her jacket—she hadn't been anywhere near hitting the ground—and took a moment to regain her dignity. When she looked up Fraser was just a couple of feet away, standing on the remains of a stone wall, his face grey.

'What?' Elspeth asked, feeling the colour drain from her own face as she took in Fraser's expression.

'I thought…'

He jumped down from the wall and strode across to her. Before she realised what was happening he had pulled her into his arms. She allowed herself to relax, to breathe him in just for a second, before remembering that she had just been reminding herself that he was off-limits. She pushed him away, and it took some strength, given his vice-like grip around her.

'Fraser, what are you doing?'

He took a deep breath—composing himself, she guessed.

'I heard a noise and I looked over and you were falling,' he said by way of explanation. Taking a step back from her now that she had disentangled herself, he started to look a little sheepish. 'I started running as soon as I saw, but I knew I wouldn't be able to get to you before you hit the ground.'

Elspeth drew her eyebrows together. 'I didn't hit the ground. It was just a little stumble.'

'But you *could* have done.'

The words burst from Fraser with unexpected force, and Elspeth guessed that he still wasn't quite in control of himself.

She forced herself to be kind, reminding herself that he had come out here full of emotions about his father that he clearly hadn't been able to handle. Reminding herself as well that he didn't have the day-to-day experience of being pregnant. Or medical training. She could see from his face that he had been genuinely scared that the baby would be hurt.

She reached out a hand and rubbed his arm in a way that she hoped would come across as comforting, rather than anything more intimate. 'I'm fine and the baby's fine. I promise. I'm sorry you were worried.'

Fraser took another deep breath, and Elspeth watched as the colour returned to his face and the expression of terror faded. And then, the drama done with, unease began to creep in as she remembered that she still hadn't quite worked out what she was going to say to Fraser when she got up here. Her somewhat melodramatic entrance onto the scene hadn't made things any less awkward.

'How did you know I was up here?' Fraser asked, and Elspeth was grateful for a question she at least knew the answer to.

'Your dad,' she said simply.

The word 'Malcolm' had been on the tip of her tongue, but at the last minute she'd changed her mind. He *was* Fraser's father, whether Fraser liked to think or speak of him that way or not. There was no point in them coming all this way if they weren't going to get to the bottom of what had happened. But if she had learnt anything from working with her patients, it was that sometimes approaching a problem sideways was more effective than hitting it head-on with a hammer. Maybe if she gave him time and opportunity Fraser would open up to her without the need for her to interrogate him.

'He said that you liked to come up here when you were a boy. He thought you might be here.'

'I love this place,' Fraser said simply, sidestepping the issue of his father. 'I always have. It was a fun playground when I was a kid.'

'I can imagine,' Elspeth said, trying to.

She looked around, looked up at the empty spaces where windows must once have kept out the wind and the rain. At dark doorways and tiny chambers that had long ago lost their walls. At nooks and crevices that had once hidden secrets and long-finished lives. She brushed a hand against a stone wall, wondering who had touched it before her. Whose lives had played out in this room. How many babies had been born and children raised here.

It was starting to hit her, she realised, why it was so important for Fraser to bring her here, for him to think of his child here. He and his family had been a part of this place for so long that it was impossible to think of them as separate. They belonged together. And understanding that made her understand how pained Fraser must be to have been so long away from this place. How much his father must have hurt him for him to stay away from so long. She had not given herself an easy task.

'Will you show me round?' she asked, hoping that her plan of giving him space and time to talk would take effect.

She'd charged up here after him because she'd been so worried about that look on his face when he'd walked out. It had been disgust and disappointment and fear, all roiling together and fighting for supremacy. But he wasn't ready to talk now. He was jumpy and sensitive and he needed to do whatever it was he did to take himself off high alert.

Fraser nodded. 'Sure.'

He climbed up to the bank where he had been standing when she had first seen him and held out a hand to help her up. He kept hold of her hand as they walked to a long stretch of great archways.

'This was the great hall. See there? That's the space where the fireplace would have been.' Stones marked out a space the size of a decent-sized kitchen on the floor. 'That would have kept the whole hall warm. And in the early days it would have been where food was cooked, ale was warmed. It was the most important place in the whole castle. Everyone lived in this room. There was no such thing as privacy as we understand it. Eating together, sleeping together…'

She could imagine what else they had all been doing in the same room, and she didn't need him to say it. In fact, she needed him *not* to say it. To be able to keep her mind as far away from sex as possible.

Elspeth spun around, her eyes tracing a sweeping arc from the flat stones on the ground in front of her up to the jagged stones at the top of the tallest tower, and back to Fraser beside her. He was looking directly at her and her gaze met his, locked with it, and she found she couldn't break it.

But she had to.

She moved her feet first, turning away from him, hoping that she'd have the strength to look away. But he caught her hand, wouldn't let her break that connection. She knew that she must be imagining the heat she could feel in her palm. The temperature was still barely above freezing, and she was wearing mittens so padded that her hands barely felt as if they belonged to her.

'I wanted you to see,' Fraser said. 'I needed you to know why this place is important.'

'It's okay,' Elspeth said soothingly, sensing something frantic, urgent, below the surface. 'I understand.'

This wasn't what she had meant. When she'd wanted him to relax she hadn't meant for him to relax into *this*. She'd come up here to talk to him about his father, and now here he was looking at her with an intensity that she knew was dangerous.

He reached for her other hand and pulled her closer. She could see the hurt in his eyes. Could see the toll that confronting things with his father was taking on him. She was sure that under the surface of this confident, sexy, close to irresistible man of thirty was a fifteen-year-old boy who was still reeling from his father leaving him.

But when his hand brushed her cheek she knew it was the man touching her, not the boy. And when he leaned in close, so that his breath was warm on her icy lips, she didn't—couldn't—care what was motivating this. Her heart was pounding with anticipation and her hands were already reaching for him when, with a sigh, his lips finally found hers.

He moved slowly at first, and she wondered—with what small part of her brain was actually functioning—whether he thought she was going to startle and bolt. God, she wished she had the strength to do that. She might think—*know*, even—that this was a bad idea, but his mouth was hot and sure and so incredibly sexy that there was no way she was ever going to want him to stop.

She wished she was wearing fewer clothes. She felt a pull deep down in her belly as Fraser's arms wrapped around her waist, lifting her up to him, and she was desperate for the feel of his skin. To get closer. To climb inside him. She pulled off a glove and grabbed a handful of his hair, crushing her body against his, desperately pushing away every reason why this was a bad idea.

Fraser's breath was coming shorter now, and her heart was pounding almost painfully in her chest. Oh, this was intoxicating. *He* was intoxicating. She remembered the first time, at the wedding, up against that tree that had pulled at her dress and grazed her skin, and how she had been so tempted to just take him right there. How did he *do* this to her?

Just as she thought that this might be it—she might never be able to stop and would die kissing this man—Fraser broke away, dragging in air as if he had just climbed a mountain.

'God, Elspeth, I don't know—'

'Don't you dare,' Elspeth said quickly, trying to catch her breath, trying to stop real life from invading the moment and making her regret it.

'Whatever you were about to say, don't. Say it later, if you have to, but don't…not just now.'

She leaned her forehead against his chest, grateful for the difference in height that meant she didn't have to look him in the eye, that meant she could gather her thoughts and her dignity without him being able to see. She couldn't even summon up any embarrassment for the way she'd responded to him. Why should she, when he'd responded as passionately as she had?

Eventually she looked up, and Fraser gave her a smile that made her want to tear his clothes off and then her own, frostbite be damned.

'Shall we walk, then?' he asked, reaching for her hand again.

She didn't have an answer. Couldn't fathom where this kiss left them now. So she walked along with him, and the knowledge that that kiss was something they couldn't take back slowly sank in. She had reacted and thought and kissed all in the moment, completely ignorant of the life-changing decision they had just made.

They couldn't forget this. Whatever happened now, she had shown him exactly what she felt for him and she couldn't take it back. They could make whatever sensible grown-up decisions they liked, but she had just proved that.

The rational part of her brain told her that some of the tension between her and Fraser should have dissipated with that kiss. He was frustrated; she was worked up. They had just been getting something out of their systems. *Yeah, right*. She knew, and she knew Fraser knew, that they had just proved that didn't work. Ignoring this hadn't made it go away. And a kiss hadn't made it go away either. Which meant…what? They were stuck with it? With each other?

For a tiny breath of a moment, she allowed herself to imagine it. That this could work. That Alex had been wrong when he had told her she was incapable of having a relationship. Perhaps she and Fraser could take this fragile new thing and protect it and nurture it until it became… She didn't know what. But until it became *something*. Something strong.

Something that would sustain her rather than drain her.

'I should apologise to my father,' Fraser said, as they walked back through the long shadows of the castle ruins.

'I think it would be a good idea. And then maybe the two of you should talk. That's what we came up here for, after all.'

'I know. I'm just still so…so angry with him.'

Elspeth squeezed his hand, knowing how hard it was for him to talk about this. How vulnerable he was making himself just by having this conversation. 'You've been angry for fifteen years,' she reminded him. 'Has it helped?'

He shook his head. 'It's not easy.'

Well, there was no point arguing with that.

'I've never expected it would be,' she said. 'You've done something incredibly brave by coming here. But do you want a relationship with him again? Do you regret losing so much time?'

Fraser nodded. 'I think you know I do.'

'Then don't lose any more,' she suggested.

She saw the words sink in. Saw that Fraser was considering them. She smiled. Fraser was letting her in. It had to be worth something that they were working through this together. It gave her hope.

'What can be done about the estate?' she asked, knowing that this was always going to be a sticking point between Fraser and Malcolm.

'I'm not sure,' Fraser said, shaking his head. 'I have cash I can invest—though I wish I'd known about this before I bought the Edinburgh apartment. Even then, though, I won't have as much as it will need. Any amount of money runs out eventually, unless you can find a way to provide an income.'

'So what's to be done?' Elspeth asked.

'This place needs money coming in. There are some things I've tried on other estates that might work. If Malcolm is willing. We need the forests better managed—the timber should be bringing in money, but they're not sustainable as they are. And then we need to get more tourists up here: sporting weekends, outdoor activities, maybe even consider opening up the castle a few days a year. Convert some of the outbuildings into luxury holiday homes. There are estates similar to this one that are thriving. But it's going to be a lot of work to turn it around.'

'Are you going to help him?' she asked, and then wondered selfishly for a moment what it would mean to her if he was. Would he want to be up here full-time? Hours away from where she and the baby would be living?

Fraser nodded. 'I haven't got a choice. I have to do it if I ever want to live here again. If I don't want it sold off before the wee one is old enough to remember it.'

They crossed the driveway and entered the tower door into the family apartments, heading for the kitchen first, and warming themselves by the range while they waited for the kettle to boil.

With a hot drink as a peace offering, they knocked on the study door and found Malcolm still poring over the spreadsheets.

Fraser pulled up a chair beside his father while Elspeth took an armchair by the fire, which Malcolm had built up while they had been gone.

As she watched Fraser and his father tiptoe

towards a truce her mind drifted back to the kiss that they had shared. If she closed her eyes she could still feel it. Feel the rasp of Fraser's stubble and the chill of his fingertips when he had touched her face. Next to the fire, she felt her body warming again, felt the pull towards sleep that had come so easily since she had been pregnant.

CHAPTER ELEVEN

FRASER GLANCED BEHIND him and saw that Elspeth's eyes had closed and she had given in to sleep. Some wingman *she* was, he thought with an affectionate smile.

He and his father had started talking about the finances again, picking up where they had left off before Fraser had walked out. But it didn't matter where he looked. All he could see was *her* name. All he wanted was an explanation.

He took a deep breath, knowing what he had to say. 'I'm sorry for leaving the way I did before. I was surprised to see that you had given Louise money, but that's no excuse.'

'Aye, well, thank you for the apology. That means a lot,' Malcolm said, leaning back in his chair with a thoughtful expression on his face. 'Reckon it's about time that we talked about her, though, son. It's been a long time.'

This time Fraser didn't bite back at the word 'son'. There was no point denying who they were to each other. And, whatever had happened since, Malcolm had been his dad, been there for him every day of the first fifteen years of his life. That earned him some rights.

'I don't understand why you're giving her money,' Fraser said, sticking to the present, not ready to fall into the past just yet. 'You can't still be financially responsible for her. You've been divorced for ten years.'

Malcolm nodded thoughtfully. 'You're right, and it's not a regular thing. But she needed to borrow a little money and I wanted to help.'

'Our home is falling down around you and you're sending *her* money?' Fraser tried to keep the anger from his voice, but he could tell from Malcolm's expression that he hadn't quite managed it.

He shrugged. 'It's only a few hundred pounds; I couldn't see what difference it would make to things here. And it's a loan. As apologies go, son, this isn't the best I've heard.'

Fraser took a deep breath, tried to control his temper so that they could actually get to the end of this conversation. Elspeth was right. Leaving so much unsaid over the years had done nothing but make him unhappy. Finishing this was going to be hard. But at least he was trying something different. Now that he could see how his anger had been eating at him all this time he wanted it gone.

'So...you're still friends, then? You and Louise? When we heard that you were divorced... I don't know. I assumed it had ended as badly as it had with Mum.'

Malcolm winced, and Fraser could see the pain and regret in his expression.

'I never meant to hurt your mother, Fraser. I wish you could believe that. Back when I met Louise and thought that I was falling in love with her I didn't want to lie to your mother, so I told her I thought we should separate. If I'd known then what I was doing...how much it would hurt her...that I would lose you...' Malcolm shook his head, looking tired. Sad. 'Love's a confusing thing, Fraser. And sometimes it makes us do—say—things we regret.'

Malcolm glanced over to where Elspeth was sleeping by the fire and Fraser wondered what he thought of their relationship. How much he had guessed about the feelings that were running between them. Well, if his father knew what was going on, Fraser would be glad of the information. Because he wasn't sure that he and Elspeth were doing such a great job between them of figuring their relationship out.

'You were only married two years,' Fraser said, accusing. 'You threw away everything that you and Mum had for something that didn't even last.'

Malcolm rubbed at his hair and sighed. 'Aye. It's easy to see that now. But at the time…'

'At the time you were only thinking about one thing.'

'Fraser…' His father's voice trailed off as he shook his head. 'That's not what happened. When I met Louise I fell in love with her. I'm sorry if it hurts you to hear that. I didn't want to lie to your mother, and so I told her what I was feeling. Louise and I were happy for a short time, but…but sometimes that's not enough. I was sad for a very long time after you left. It's hard for a relationship to survive that.'

'You chose *her*,' Fraser said, the words tearing at his throat.

It was the thought that had haunted him for so many years. The fact that he hadn't been good enough for his father. That he hadn't been enough. That his father hadn't chosen *him*.

'I didn't know at the time, Fraser, that that was what I was choosing. I know that's what you threatened, but I thought you would come round. That if I gave you space you would change your mind. I didn't know what to do. I always wanted you to come home, but I didn't know how to talk to you.'

Malcolm leaned forward, but Fraser moved away on instinct, needing to keep some distance. Everything his father was saying… It was making him question everything he'd thought he'd known about his past. About himself.

'You moved Louise in here when I was barely out of the door.'

Fraser held up his hands in defeat. 'You were a child, Fraser, and so angry. I didn't know what to do.'

'I just wanted you to choose *me*!' Fraser exclaimed, and then glanced across to make sure that he hadn't woken Elspeth. 'I wanted me and Mum to be more important than she was. I wanted our life together, what you had with us, to be more important than what you thought you might have with her.'

His father sank into his chair. 'If I'd known, son, that I wouldn't see you for so long, that you really meant it, I wouldn't have done it. I would do anything to go back and make a different choice.'

Fraser looked into his father's face and for the first time felt ashamed. He saw that he had brought as much pain to his father as he had felt himself over the years. If either one of them had compromised perhaps they both could have been spared some pain.

'It's not too late,' Malcolm said, reading the mood and placing a hand over Fraser's. 'There's a new life on the way and I hope—'

Malcolm's voice cracked, and Fraser swallowed down an answering lump in his throat.

'I hope that this is the start of something. I would so love to get to know you again, Fraser. To meet my grandchild and watch him grow up.'

'Aye,' Fraser said eventually, not trusting himself with a longer word. After several deep breaths he lifted his head and looked his father in the eye. 'I'd like that too,' he said, with a small nod that sealed the matter.

CHAPTER TWELVE

'DO YOU—?'

'Should we—?'

Elspeth laughed nervously, feeling the door-knob cool and smooth beneath her hand as she started again. 'I think we should probably talk about what happened earlier,' she said.

After she had woken alone in the study and gone to find Fraser and Malcolm, Elspeth had been astonished to discover them at the table in the kitchen, papers strewn between them and an animated conversation in flow. She had wondered if she'd woken in some sort of parallel universe. But the two men had been full of plans, looking to the future of Ballanross.

They had all spent a lively afternoon around that table, playing with different ideas, making suggestions for new business ventures. And it had only been as they'd left the kitchen late in the evening that there had been space to think, never mind talk about the kiss that had happened earlier.

As she had turned the brass knob on her bedroom door she'd paused, knowing in that moment that she absolutely did not want to sleep on it alone. To let whatever had captured them that morning dissipate overnight or become too big to talk about. She'd opened her mouth to speak, only Fraser had too.

Now she took a deep breath, deciding to be brave, and to say what she had been thinking all day: 'I think we need to talk about what happened earlier. We're meant to be just friends, Fraser. I can't be in a relationship—not with all the other responsibilities in my life. But all the time we're either snapping at each other or—'

'Kissing each other?'

She tried to hide her smile, not wanting Fraser to know how the memory of that kiss lit her up from the inside.

'Or trying really hard not to.'

He snorted, gave a little huff of laughter. 'Hmmph, thanks for the ego-boost.'

She opened the door behind her and glanced back over her shoulder as she crossed the threshold to make sure that Fraser had read her invitation and followed.

Elspeth pulled the heavy velvet curtains before sitting down on the stiff upholstered bench in front of the window. 'I'm clearly not doing a great job.'

'I'm glad you stopped trying,' Fraser replied as he joined her.

'Who said I stopped?'

She ducked her head as he stared at her, not wanting him to know how she was feeling. It had been hard enough to resist him when her memories from the wedding were faded and dog-eared and starting to feel as if they could have happened to someone else. The memory of this morning was so sharp and Technicolor that her mind could have her back in the moment faster than she could blink.

'That helps,' he said, brushing one hand across her cheek. 'If everything that happened this morning was while you were *trying* to resist me I'd like to see what happens when you really let yourself go.'

She couldn't help the smile turning up the corners of her lips, and she gave him a look to remind him that he knew exactly what happened when she let down her guard with him. The widening of his eyes and the slight flush to his skin let her know that she'd hit her mark.

She felt herself leaning in to him, drawn to him as if she had no control over her own body. But she couldn't let that distract her—again. She pulled herself back into line. She wasn't just some slave to her hormones. She was going to be a mother: she had to get her life in order. She moved away, leaving Fraser with his lips moistened and fire in his eyes.

'Don't be sensible,' he said, reading her perfectly.

'We have to be,' she replied, glancing down at her bump, knowing that he would understand what she was thinking. He was developing an uncanny knack for that. 'We're meant to be talking.'

'I don't want to talk. I want to—'

She touched his lips with the tips of her fingers, stopping the words before they could be said.

'Don't say it. If you say it I might change my mind. We've been pretending we can will these feelings to disappear. We've done a terrible job, so we need a new plan.'

Fraser leaned away from her slightly. From the thoughtful look on his face, he seemed to be assessing how serious she was about this. Could he be playful and kiss her—or was this talk non-negotiable.

'Does there always have to be a plan?' he asked.

'Yes!'

Fraser visibly started at the bite in her tone, but to his credit didn't push her on it. Well, at least she'd answered his unspoken question, as well as the one he'd asked out loud. There was to be no kissing on the agenda until they'd talked about what happened earlier.

'Okay,' he said, speaking softly and slowly, as if trying to calm a skittish horse. 'Then how about this for a plan?'

He cupped her cheek, his hand moving as slowly as his words, and just as she was about to push him away he paused and flicked his gaze up to her eyes from her mouth. But he didn't kiss her. Didn't cross the invisible line that she had drawn between them.

'I think about this all day,' he said. 'It's exhausting trying to deny it. To deny myself.'

Elspeth heaved in a deep breath, sending it down to her fingertips to stop them grabbing at him—to her mouth, to stop it begging him to deliver on what that look had just promised.

'It doesn't leave me time or energy for anything else. Maybe if we stopped fighting. Maybe if we...'

She thought he was going to do it—to lean in and complete this kiss. He was going to make their bed and she would enjoy lying in it.

But he just rested his forehead against hers. 'Maybe, if we weren't putting so much effort into fighting so damn hard, things would work themselves out.'

'But...' Elspeth started to say. She had so many sensible objections that she didn't even know where to start. She couldn't be in a relationship. There was too much at stake. If she were distracted by Fraser and something happened to Sarah she would never be able to forgive herself.

'I know… I know,' Fraser said, lifting her hand back to his lips for a gentle kiss. 'There's a million reasons why this might not work. Why it would make more sense for us to resist. But I can't help feeling that if I weren't expending so much energy *resisting* you every second of the day, maybe we'd find the answer to making this work. Could that be our plan? We stop fighting against what we want and see what happens.'

What if he was right? She was thinking about him all day anyway—when she was at work, when she was with Sarah, when she was in the car, when she should be sleeping. Thinking about how she was going to resist him. Thinking about that night after the wedding. Thinking about all the reasons why this was a bad idea. If all that went away, would she have *more* time for everything else in her life, rather than less?

'Watchful waiting…' Elspeth said thoughtfully.

Fraser frowned. 'What?'

At last she met his eyes. 'It's doctor-speak for wait and see. For observing how something progresses before you decide whether you need to intervene or not.'

Fraser nodded, reflecting her smile back at her. He was still so close she could feel his breath on her lips. Still not taking that choice from her.

'Watchful waiting,' he echoed. 'I like the sound of that. Though the waiting part sounds a lot like what we've been doing already.'

A surge of heat started in the pit of her belly and spread up over her chest, until she was sure her cheeks were flaming. 'I can't wait for you much longer, I don't think,' she said, being honest at last. 'I'm not sure I've got the strength.'

He gave her a look that burned and melted her at the same time, like a candle, puddling wax around its own flame.

'You're the strongest woman I—'

She pressed her lips against his and it lit her up as it had the last time, the first time, every time she had kissed him. But with the urgency of knowing she shouldn't be doing this gone, she felt something else in his kiss, a sweetness, a tenderness that had been drowned out before.

Or, she wondered, maybe this was new. Maybe this was deeper.

With her eyes closed, she brought her hand to his face, rubbed her thumb against the fullness of his bottom lip, rediscovering the contours of his mouth, taking the time to relearn every line.

The night of the wedding, and in the dreams she had had since, he was a silhouetted shape in the half-light. He was the desire and the urgency that had made her lose her inhibitions and led her into trouble. Now the urgency had gone, had been replaced with something richer. She didn't need to consume this experience in one sitting, knowing that she wouldn't have another chance. She could take her time over this. Indulge every curiosity. She could stop and enjoy every moment with each of her senses. And she intended to.

'Enjoying yourself?' Fraser asked, as her explorations continued.

'Mmm…' Elsepth replied as she trailed kisses along his jaw, pressed her lips to the soft, sensitive skin behind his ear.

His lips dropped to her collarbone, nudging

aside the fabric of her sweater, sending a shock of desire right through her. His cold hands on her waist made her jump, and she pulled away.

'What's the hurry?' she asked, acting innocent.

Fraser held his hands up in supplication. 'If you want to be in charge…'

He leaned back and turned his head, pulling her on top of him so she could carry on where she'd left off—except he'd clearly forgotten the football-sized bump between them, and she let out an *oomph* as she landed on him and the breath was squeezed from her.

Fraser lifted his head in alarm, propping himself up on his elbows. 'Did I hurt you? Are you okay?'

'I'm fine,' Elspeth said, pushing him back on the bench seat, lowering herself gently until she was lying on top of him. 'Things have changed a wee bit since we were last here. That's all.'

He ran his hands over her bump and smiled at her appreciatively.

'You look beautiful,' he said, pulling her face down for another kiss with one hand. The other still rested possessively on her belly. 'And you feel incredible. All full and tight and about to burst. It's been impossible to ignore how sexy you are like this.'

She laughed, kissing him back. 'The hormones must have gone to your head. But I'll take it.' She resumed her explorations, and this time didn't protest as his hands found their way under her clothes and over her skin.

There was no light around the edges of the curtains when Elspeth's phone rang the next morning. That didn't mean much in the Highlands in winter—it could be nine in the morning or three in the afternoon. So she glanced at the time on her phone as she picked it up—five in the morning.

She felt a frisson of dread familiar to anyone living with chronic illness and disability in their lives when a phone rang in the middle of the night. Her mother's name was on the screen. Elspeth swallowed her fear down, not wanting her mother to hear that she was worried.

'Mum? Everything okay?' she asked in a

whisper, not wanting to wake Fraser, snoring softly beside her.

Elspeth held her breath as her mum spoke. She had fallen in the shower and had to call an ambulance. She was in A&E now, which meant that the respite carer they'd booked was at home with Sarah, unsupervised.

'I'll come home right away,' Elspeth said, calculating driving times in her head. 'Don't worry. I'll be back in a few hours.'

She ignored her mum's protests—because what else could she do? She wasn't going to risk having someone underqualified and inexperienced taking care of Sarah when she could be back there herself in a few hours, making sure that everything was done exactly as it needed to be.

A *hmmmph* beside her in the bed let her know that Fraser was awake and unhappy about it. One of his hands curved around her hip, but she pushed it away. This wouldn't have happened if she hadn't come up here with him, she thought to herself. She wouldn't be sitting here wondering what might happen to Sarah if the agency had sent someone inexperienced, imagining all the worst-case scenarios that haunted her late at night when she thought about strangers looking after her sister.

She crept from under the blankets, hoping Fraser would fall back to sleep before remembering that she didn't have her car here and she'd need him to drive her home.

'What's going on?' he asked, lifting himself on to one elbow and eyeing her suspiciously as she flicked on a light and started throwing things into her suitcase. 'Elspeth?' he said, trepidation in his voice. 'Are ye going somewhere?'

'There's an emergency at home,' she said, without looking round. 'I've got to go and take care of my sister. I'm sorry. I know we meant to stay longer. Perhaps I could take the car and—'

Fraser sat up properly, pushing the hair out of his eyes, still not looking one hundred per cent awake.

'No, I'll drive you, Elspeth. Of course I will. Is Sarah okay? Your mum?'

'Mum's had a fall. She's in A&E waiting for

X-rays—which means Sarah's home alone with the carer.'

'I'm sorry about your mum. But is there no one else who can help out? Someone closer?'

That's just what Alex would say.

The thought appeared in her brain before she could stop it.

'I really have to go, Fraser. I know it's not what we planned, but that's just the way it is.'

Fraser glanced around the room, trying to guess from the light—or lack of it—what time it was. From the grit in his eyes and the ache in his muscles he guessed that it wasn't much later than when they had finally fallen asleep.

'It's not about what we planned, Elspeth,' he said, trying to catch up with what was happening, trying to stave off the fear that she was about to walk out on him. 'It was an innocent question. I'm trying to understand what's going on.'

She stopped packing and stood still for a moment. 'Look, I know you're not used to this. But this is how it is with my family—

my life. Sometimes I have to drop everything and just go.'

She was moving round the room purposefully, pulling on clothes, throwing others sharply into her suitcase. It was clear that she was leaving. Had she given him a moment's consideration or was she just going to lift his keys and go?

'This is exactly what I was worried about, coming up here. This is exactly why I've said all along that this won't work.'

'And would you be running so fast if it wasn't for last night?' he asked, knowing that he was entering dangerous waters. Last night they had found such a fragile balance…she had taken such a risk by giving in to what she wanted. What they *both* wanted. Was she regretting it now?

'What's that supposed to mean?' Elspeth asked, but it was clear from the way she refused to meet his eyes that she knew.

'Exactly what you think it means,' he said, his voice growing cold as the fear that she was walking away from him sank in. 'This would be a very convenient exit route if you regret what happened last night. If you've changed your mind about watchful waiting and want to take action instead.'

'If I had been at home last night none of this would have happened,' Elspeth said plainly, finally meeting his gaze with a stony expression.

Fraser rose from the bed and came over to her, bringing the thick bedspread with him and wrapping it around them both. 'Everything's going to be okay,' he said, kissing her on the lips and praying that she would respond.

She softened a little and warmed under his touch, her mouth moving gently against his as he pulled her closer, holding on tight.

But as he deepened the kiss she pushed him away. 'We should go,' she said when they broke apart, her expression cold.

When she had kissed him, the fear had receded a little, but it was rushing back now. 'When do you need to leave?' he asked.

Elspeth glanced at her phone, checking the time. 'As soon as we can.'

She breathed a sigh of relief when he nodded.

He sat on the bed for another few moments, watching Elspeth pack. What had happened in this room while he had been sleeping? He'd closed his eyes late last night—early this morning?—with Elspeth breathing warm and soft on his chest and her bump pressing gently against his hip. And he had woken to an empty bed and the beginnings of the relationship they'd worked so hard for looking more fragile than ever.

He knocked on his father's bedroom door, his bags in his hand, and explained what was happening, and then they were crunching across the driveway, trying to get some heat into the car, chase the ice from the windows.

He glanced across at her as he drove, watched her withdraw into silence, and he wanted to pull her into his arms. Everything seemed so much simpler when he was touching her.

He reached for her hand and gripped it tight, trying to show her how much he wanted this to work. 'It'll be okay, you know,' he said, trying to start up the conversation that had gone cold back in her bedroom.

'You don't know that,' she said, her voice devoid of emotion. 'You *can't* know that. You don't understand.'

He didn't know what to say to that. Didn't know how to reach her now she had decided to shut him out. No, he didn't understand her—because she wouldn't let him in. He wanted to know her. Wanted to be a part of her life, a part of her family. But *she* needed to want that too. He couldn't support her if she wouldn't let him.

Finally they pulled up outside the home that she shared with her mother and her sister and he turned to look at her. Wondering if, at last, she would find some explanation for what was happening between them. Give him some hope that this wasn't going the direction he feared.

She had pushed him hard this weekend, forcing him to face up to the decisions—the mistakes—he had made in his life. And he'd worked hard to reach a point where he could picture himself with someone. Moving towards those big, scary feelings that had always had him running scared in the past.

And now what? Was she going to prove that he had been right all along? That he would have been better never getting involved with her?

'Thank you for driving me back,' she said, as if she were reading from a script, and reached for the door handle.

Fraser sighed, opened his own door, and then pulled her bags from the back of the car and brought them round to where she was standing on the pavement, digging through her handbag for her keys.

He dropped the bags at her feet, and before she could protest cupped a hand around her cheek.

'Please,' he said. 'Don't decide anything now. Don't go into your head and make this go away. I'll stop by tonight and we can talk.'

She hesitated, but he pressed a gentle kiss to her cheek.

'Remember this,' he instructed, his voice low, his breath on her ear, unable to drag himself away from her. 'Remember last night. Remember what we are to each other when we are together like this. This feeling—it's important. Don't give up on it yet.'

She closed her eyes and took a deep breath, and for a moment Fraser thought she would turn him down. Again. Instead she tensed her shoulders. Looked up and met his gaze.

'Okay. Let's talk tonight.'

CHAPTER THIRTEEN

ELSPETH SAT IN the quiet house, her hand resting on her bump, trying to take stock of the last twenty-four hours. When they'd driven up to the Highlands such a short time ago she had been so sure that a relationship with Fraser—with anyone—was nothing short of impossible. Then, last night, it had seemed inevitable.

But she had watched the sun rise as they had clocked up the miles this morning and her certainty, her faith in her decision had faltered. Now she was sitting here knowing that when Fraser returned she would break their relationship off, and feeling unsure of how she would live with herself when the deed was done.

As soon as they'd got back, Elspeth had jumped straight in with Sarah's daily routine—taking the splints off Sarah's hands and legs, teasing out her tight muscles with gentle wiggles and hard stretches that made her wince.

Elspeth had soothed Sarah through it, as she always did. She knew exactly how hard she could press and pull, which fingers would be most painful to straighten, when Sarah would need a break to catch her breath, with an understanding and an intimacy that an agency carer could never reproduce.

Now she had helped Sarah to shower and dress, brushed her hair and vacuumed her wheelchair, Elspeth still needed to keep busy. She'd hoped she could spend an hour chatting with her sister, but Sarah needed to study and had asked Elspeth to leave her in peace.

Fraser had asked her not to make any rash decisions, but what else could she do? The one night she'd decided to take a risk she had been called home for an emergency. She couldn't have asked for a clearer sign about the viability of their relationship.

She could hear what Alex would have said as clearly as if he were back in this house with her—*You choose them over me every time.* Of course she did. Because the risks if she made a different choice were unacceptably high. When Sarah had been born Elspeth had sat by her cot for months, willing her to get better, to come home. She never wanted to feel so helpless again, and if that meant she had to sacrifice her own relationships to be there for her sister, it would be worth it.

That last argument with Alex, when she had chosen her family for the last time and broken off their engagement, it had been such a relief. Alex had pushed her and pushed her to choose. Every time she'd had to cancel a date or cut short a holiday he'd rolled his eyes and she'd seen his judgement. And when he'd told her that he wouldn't move in with her mum and her sister she'd known they didn't have a future.

She didn't want to do that again. Didn't want to watch the novelty fade from a relationship, see love sour because she couldn't give what her partner was demanding from her.

She could tell herself that it would be different with Fraser. That he wasn't Alex. That he wouldn't expect her to choose, as Alex had. She *could* tell herself that—if she didn't already know that Fraser was the sort of uncompromising man who had been issuing ultimatums since he was a teenager.

When his dad hadn't been prepared to drop everything else because Fraser had demanded it, he hadn't spoken to him for fifteen years. This wasn't a man who was going to be happy settling for the small part of herself that she had to offer. It would be better for him to find someone who could give him the undivided love he wanted and deserved.

Elspeth cupped her hands around her belly. She loved her mum and Sarah more than she could say. And she knew she was going to love her baby with a fierce, limitless passion. She simply couldn't see how she could love Fraser like that too.

Except her heart hurt as if she did already. As if she loved him with her whole heart, with no room for anyone else. As if she'd be left cold and empty if she had to give him up.

She thought of a future of polite exchanges as they handed the baby over every other weekend. Of calling to pass on information about doctor's appointments or school reports. And then she thought how much worse it would be if *he* broke it off instead. If she loved all these people and made it work and then had Fraser tell her that she wasn't doing it well enough. As Alex had done. If he told her that the part of herself she was offering just wasn't enough for him. It would break her heart, she knew. In a way that couldn't be fixed.

When Fraser's knock on the door sounded that evening, after her mum had gone to bed to rest after her long day at the hospital and her sister had returned to her room after dinner to study, Elspeth had made up her mind and firmed her resolve. She opened the door and braced herself for the sight of him, knowing that her body would react, trying to get it in line before she did something she couldn't take back.

She spotted the flowers in his hand and shook her head, smiling slightly at the sweet gesture. Another reminder of what a man she was giving up.

'Fraser, you shouldn't have…' she started, her voice trailing off.

He leaned in and planted a kiss on her cheek. 'I didn't,' he replied, mirroring her smile.

'They're for your mum. I wanted to make a good impression, under the circumstances…'

'The circumstances being you impregnating me before you'd been properly introduced to my family?' she said with a raised eyebrow. 'I didn't realise they did flowers for that.'

Fraser smiled. 'You should see the poem in the card.'

She smiled back despite herself, despite knowing what she had to do, and stood aside to let him in.

'Come through to the kitchen. I'll find a vase for them.'

She stood and fussed with the flowers, hoping that somehow something would happen to make this easier. That she would wake up with it magically having been done for her. But as Fraser tried to catch her eye—to connect with her—she knew that she wasn't that lucky. She was going to have to live through every tortuous moment of this.

'Did everything go okay today?' Fraser asked. 'With your mum at the hospital?'

'Mmm…' Elspeth replied, building up her courage.

She couldn't engage in small talk. If she did that it would be too easy to be pulled back from what she knew she had to do. To chicken out.

'Fraser, I'm sorry, but I can't do this. We can't be together. It's never going to work. I have too many responsibilities, and it's only going to be worse when the baby gets here. We should just end it now, before we get any further in.'

Fraser nodded slowly, and she could practically see the machinations of his thinking as he tried to choose words that would make her change her mind.

'How have things changed since last night?' he asked eventually.

She leant back against the worktop, her weight pressing through her palms as she closed her eyes and fought the memories.

'Everything has changed since then.'

Fraser took a step towards her. 'I don't see how.'

'What happened this morning—'

'Has happened a hundred times before,' Fraser interrupted her. 'You told me that. And it'll probably happen a hundred times again. You knew that when we went to bed together last night.'

She threw her hands up. 'Yes, but—'

He thought he understood, but he didn't. He didn't know the strain that it put on a relationship. He hadn't lived through it already. She had. She knew where this was going before it had even got started.

'But what?' Fraser asked, maddeningly calm in his refusal to understand her or believe her.

'But I forgot,' she said, hoping that he wouldn't see the truth. That she'd known and remembered every reason why it might not work but none of that had seemed as important as the fact that she loved him.

She'd watched Fraser and his father put to rest fifteen years of pain and hurt and recrimination. And she'd thought, *I want that. If I love him enough, maybe I can have that*. But she'd forgotten that his problems stemmed from the past. Her problems were right now. They were happening today. And loving him, seeing him ready to love, didn't change *her* circumstances, however much she wanted it to be true.

'Maybe I just gave in,' she said. Not wanting him to guess how she really felt. 'Or I was kidding myself that I could do this. That I could be enough. But I can't. There's not enough of me to go around, Fraser.'

'Not enough? Elspeth, you're making so many assumptions here. You're telling me I can't have something I haven't even asked for. All I want is to talk about this. Why won't you do that?'

'Because I've talked this thing to death, Fraser. I've talked and talked and talked and the grand conclusion is that I can't do both. I can't be the daughter and sister that I need to be—*I want* to be—and be a good enough girlfriend as well.'

Fraser narrowed his eyes as he looked at her. 'You've talked about it with who? Because you haven't talked about it with *me*. And I'd have thought my opinion should count for something.'

She hesitated, but Fraser fixed her with a glare and wouldn't back down.

She shrugged in resignation. She might as well tell him. 'With Alex—my ex.'

'The one who called off the wedding?'

'*I* called off the wedding,' she said. The distinction was important.

Silence fell over the kitchen as she waited for her words to sink in.

'Why?'

Fraser said it in a way that she knew meant he wasn't going to take any bull. He would know if she was lying to him. If she wasn't being completely honest. And, really, he might as well know. This would be the final nail in the coffin of this relationship—if she could even call it that before it had really got started. There was no way he'd want her after this.

'Because he always wanted more than I could give. The part of my life that he occupied was never enough for him. He was insisting that after the wedding we would get our own place. My mum and sister said they were fine with it, but the closer it got, the less I wanted to leave. I *like* being here with them. I *like* it that if there's an emergency in the middle of the night I'm here to deal with it. I *like* it that my sister knows whether I need comfort carbs or a massive bowl of ice cream based on nothing more than the tone of my voice. But Alex wouldn't budge. He said if we were going to be married it was time to get our own place. I had to choose.'

She saw the realisation hit Fraser in stages, slowly sinking in. She'd been given an ultimatum. She'd made the choice he'd wanted his father to make. She'd do it again if she had to, and she wouldn't choose Fraser. He was second choice—again. Or that was how he would see it.

'I'm sorry, Fraser. It won't work. We were crazy to think that it could. I'm sorry.'

'You apologised already. Save it.'

Anger spiked in her. He was acting as if this was a *free* choice. It wasn't. Who would *choose* to feel this way?

'What would you have me do, Fraser? Should I choose you? Should I let my mother and Sarah and my patients fend for themselves while I go up to Ballanross and soothe your ego? You gave your dad an ultimatum and you've been punishing him for fifteen years for choosing love over his family. This is an impossible situation.'

'I'm not asking you to choose,' Fraser said, his voice raised and his tone frustrated. 'The opposite. I'm asking you to try and do both. To find space in your life for me. To make room for me.'

'I did that before and—'

'But not with *me*! So it didn't work out before. Why does that mean it won't work this time? I'm not Alex. I'm not asking you for more than you can give. I'm standing here telling you that I'll take anything you're willing to give me, and you're telling me that you're not even going to try.'

She shook her head. This pig-headed man was just refusing to get this. Out of spite. Out of… She didn't know why he was refusing to understand something so simple.

'I'm sorry, Fraser, but we both know you're the kind of guy who hands out ultimatums. You did it to your father and you'll do it to me. And I just can't go through that again.'

'Why are you so convinced that I'm the same as your ex? Can't you accept that I'm different? That *we* will be different? That the choices in front of you are different this time? I understand your being scared. What I don't understand is why you're not even willing to try.'

Well, at least she knew the answer to that one. 'Because trying is exhausting, Fraser. And I can't do it any more. It's just not worth it.'

CHAPTER FOURTEEN

HE WASN'T WORTH IT.

She'd given him the answer that he'd dreaded hearing since they had started this journey. Well, he didn't know much about her experiences with men and relationships, but he knew that he'd had a lot of women over the years and not one of them had made him question the way he was living his life. And then he'd met her. He might not be worth fighting for, but she was—and he wasn't giving up yet.

There was something special between them. Something rare and precious. There had to be. It was something he didn't want to lose. And if she didn't feel that way too she wouldn't have gone to bed with him last night.

He took a couple of steps towards her, until he was standing close enough to touch her if she'd let him, one foot either side of hers. She didn't move—not towards him or away—and he could read the indecision on her face. She wanted this. She wanted him. But she wasn't going to let that be enough.

He placed a hand beside one of hers on the edge of the worktop and with the knuckles of his other hand gently stroked her cheek. He moved slowly, not wanting to spook her. Not wanting to push her to do anything she didn't want to. He pulled her towards him, resting his forehead against hers.

'This is different,' he said, hoping above all that he was right about this one thing. Hoping that she felt something when they touched that she hadn't felt before. He was betting everything on it. 'Did it feel like this before?' he asked, letting his body sink towards her, his stomach pressing on her bump, feeling their baby growing there between them. 'With him? Or is this different? Am *I* different?'

Elspeth sighed. He felt the breath leave her body in a long, resigned wave, and for a moment he thought that was it. He was wrong. This wasn't different for her. But then she turned her cheek into his hand—just a fraction.

A movement so subtle he might have missed it if he hadn't been desperately looking for any sign that she was still with him on this.

'It's not going to work, Fraser.'

'That's not what I asked.' Fraser allowed himself a tiny glimmer of hope that this wasn't a hard no, that she had evaded rather than answered his question. 'I asked if I'm different.'

She paused again, and tensed slightly beneath him.

'You are,' she conceded, glancing up and briefly meeting his gaze.

'And you *feel* different,' Fraser prompted, building on her concession, moving her towards what he was sure was true. 'You feel different from how you felt with Alex.'

She held her breath and he could practically *hear* her looking for the get-out. For a way of denying what they were both realising had to be true.

'Yes.'

The word was barely more than a breath, but to Fraser it was everything. It was hope. It was life. It was all he needed to know to keep going. She had pushed him and pushed him to face up to his past, to address the problems with his father that he had carried into every adult relationship he had ever made. And now he was going to do the same for her. He was going to make her see that she could do this. She *could* be enough. She could be everything she needed to be to her family, and whatever was left for her to offer him he would take it.

'Then we're going to try.' His voice rang with the certainty that he felt. 'This isn't the same. You don't have to be the person you were when you were with Alex. I'm not asking you to tear yourself in different directions. All I'm asking—*all* I'm asking—is that you don't write this off.'

He softened his hand and stroked her cheek with his thumb, trying with everything he had not to rush her. To give her time to think. To stop himself from breaching those last few centimetres between his lips and hers. To give her space to come to him when she was ready.

'I can't live at Ballanross,' she said, and he pulled back, surprised.

Of all the responses he'd thought she might give, that one had never occurred to him.

'I can't even live in your new apartment.'

'I never asked you to,' he reminded her.

'But I couldn't. I won't. And you would want to. Not now, perhaps. But eventually you'll want to go back to Ballanross.'

How many hypotheticals was she going to run through? How many times was she going to assume the worst of him? This relationship was never going to move forward if she couldn't see that this wasn't her last relationship. That he wasn't Alex.

'I'd like to spend time there, yes. If that's something that we can do,' Fraser said, keeping his cool even as Elspeth was losing hers. 'And there's plenty of room for your mum and your sister, if we ever want to live there. If that's what we all choose. But I don't need to.'

He realised the truth of what he was saying as the words left his mouth. 'I would choose *you*, Elspeth, if it came to it.'

The realisation that he meant it hit him like a truck. All these years he'd dreamed of going back to his home. All this time the castle had loomed large in his memory. But it had only been a symbol of what he had lost. Of what he was missing. It had never been about the castle. And he wasn't going to choose a symbol over the woman he loved. He would be wherever she was. For ever. If she would let him.

'I'm not asking—' Elspeth started to say.

He cut her off, because she didn't need to say it. 'I know you're not. Because you're not the sort of idiot who gives ultimatums to the people you love. But it's true anyway. I can live with never going back there. But I couldn't live without you. Without our baby. I want us to be a family—together—and I'll do that in the city if that's what it takes to make you agree. To make you happy.'

What would make her happy?

She couldn't remember the last time she'd asked herself that question. The last time she had made a free choice rather than weighing up all the opposing forces in her life and trying to pick the least bad option.

But Fraser was asking something different. He wasn't asking what she *didn't* want. He wasn't asking her what the lesser of all the evils was. He was asking her, as no one had done for a really long time, what she *wanted.*

And there could only be one answer. She wanted him. She wanted him in her life, in her family, in her bed. She wanted him any way she could get him, and she wanted him now. But that didn't mean she could have him.

'Elspeth? I hope you're not about to do something stupid!' Sarah shouted from the other side of the kitchen door.

Elspeth shook her head in dismay. How long had she been there listening?

'Did no one ever tell you it's rude to eavesdrop?' Elspeth shouted back, leaning against the counter and letting out a sigh. She walked over and opened the door, stepping out of the way before Sarah could catch her toes with her powered wheelchair.

'You must have forgotten to teach me that one. Now, is there a good reason why you're not jumping on him?' Sarah asked with a raised eyebrow. 'I mean given how in love with him you are and everything.' She turned to Fraser. 'Don't let her tell you that she needs to look after us. I've been telling her for years that she needs to get over it.'

'In love with me, are you?' Fraser asked, looking from Sarah to Elspeth, raising his eyebrows.

Elspeth bristled, and decided the safest thing to do was to ignore the question. Safer to stick to the practical considerations—they came with easy answers. Talking about moving out and it actually being a viable possibility were two very different things. Something her sister didn't seem to grasp.

'*Getting over it* is easier said than done.' Elspeth busied herself filling the kettle and flicking the switch, needing something to do with her hands, somewhere to look other than at Fraser. 'Especially as you do actually *need* me here, Sarah.'

'Well, I'm going to move out when I finish college anyway,' Sarah said. 'You'll have loads more free time then.'

Fraser drew his eyebrows together in surprise as he looked over at Sarah. 'Sounds exciting,' he said. 'Elspeth didn't mention that.'

But Elspeth was shaking her head. She had

been through this with Sarah so many times before. It just wasn't realistic for her to live alone. Sure, there were other people in Sarah's position who managed, but she didn't want her sister to just *manage.* She wanted her to have the best care. That meant Elspeth doing as much of it as possible herself. And that only worked if they were living together.

'You can't do that, Sarah. We've been through all this already.'

'Don't tell me I can't. I can employ a team of assistants and carers. Plenty of people do it. I'm not having you martyr yourself for me.'

Elspeth poured hot water into the teapot and then slammed it down on the counter, harder than she'd intended. 'I'm not martyring myself. I *want* to take care of you.'

'But that's not what Sarah wants,' Fraser said, glancing from one sister to the other. 'I think we need to talk about that. About why you're trying to keep your sister dependent on you.'

'You never stop,' Sarah added. 'Even when it's making you miserable.'

'Caring for you doesn't make me *miserable*, Sarah. How could you think that?'

Tears prickled at the back of Elspeth's eyes at the idea that Sarah could think that. She *loved* looking after her sister. And as for what Fraser had said—he couldn't possibly understand the relationship between her and Sarah. This wasn't his call to make, however much he might like to feel in control of the situation.

'Maybe it's not making you miserable,' Fraser conceded, 'but it's stopping you from giving our relationship a chance.'

Sarah smiled at Fraser. 'Did I mention that I really like this guy, Elspeth? He's right. Being apart from Fraser is making you miserable. And you *do* know, don't you, that if I move out I'm not going to suddenly drop dead?'

Fraser pulled up a chair and sat at the table. 'Look, we don't need to make any decisions about this now. If we all want to live together, we can make that happen. Sarah, if you want to live on your own I'm sure we will support you.'

Elspeth looked from one to the other, wondering when they had decided to gang up on her.

'Are you telling me that I'm making it all

up?' Elspeth asked seriously. 'That I've *imagined* that I've needed to do everything I have? Because you don't remember, Sarah, what it was like when you were born. When I was terrified every day that you might die. When I had to remind Mum to eat because the only thing she could think about was getting you through the day.'

Elspeth brought the tea over to the table, and Sarah reached out to touch her hand.

'Of course you haven't made it up. You know Mum and I couldn't have managed without you. But we want you to be happy. If we'd known that the way things are makes you think you can't have your own life too we'd *never* have let it go on this long. Is this why you and Alex broke up?'

Sarah glanced at Fraser, obviously worried that she was oversharing in front of the new guy.

'I know about Alex,' Fraser said, his expression making it clear that he wasn't a fan.

'Well, that's good.' Sarah nodded approvingly. 'But, Elspeth, if you think that you split up because you didn't want to move out, then you've missed something important. You split up because he wasn't prepared to have this conversation with you. Fraser's not doing too badly so far…'

Elspeth could feel Fraser's eyes on her, trying to judge her reaction.

'Anyway,' Sarah said at last, 'if you put my tea in my bottle I'll leave you two to it. Oh, and Mum and I have booked a carer for the morning. So don't you *dare* use me as an excuse not to… Well… You get the idea.'

And with that parting shot Sarah left the room, leaving a heavy silence in her wake.

'Your sister wants to move out?' Fraser said, breaking the silence. 'You never told me that.'

Elspeth shook her head. There was a good reason for that. 'No, because it's not happening.'

'How does *that* work?'

Fraser came to stand in front of her and her whole body hummed with the awareness of knowing she could just reach out and touch him.

'Surely if she's an adult she gets to decide for herself.'

'Or maybe she should listen to her *doctor* sister when she tells her it's not a great idea.'

Fraser crossed his arms and narrowed his eyes. 'You don't *want* her to be independent?'

'Of course I do! I bend over backwards helping her to be independent. I don't want her to—'

She stopped herself, suddenly aware that the sentence had nearly got away from her.

'Finish the sentence,' Fraser prompted her gently. 'Come on—we were getting somewhere. You don't want her to…what?'

'I don't want her to *die*,' Elspeth said, her voice breaking.

'And is that likely to happen?' Fraser asked gently. 'If Sarah's care comes from somewhere else—like she says she wants? Does that make it more likely? Because *she* said that's not going to happen. Is she wrong?'

Her objective doctor brain provided the answer. 'No, she isn't.'

'Then why is it so hard to let her go?' he asked gently.

Elspeth thought about it for a second. Considered dodging the question. But she had been carrying this around for so long. Trying to make sense of her life. Trying to make the best of it. But it hadn't made her happy. It wasn't making Sarah happy. It wasn't going to make Fraser happy either. Maybe it was time that she started telling the truth.

'Because I've been scared that she might die for as long as I can remember. Since I was a little girl and she was born and there was nothing I could do except sit by her and hope that she wouldn't. I studied hard and I went to uni and I became a doctor because I didn't want to feel helpless. And now I can *do* something about it.'

The thought of living without her sister was unbearably painful. The thought of sitting and doing nothing was almost as bad.

'And what do you think would happen if you stopped?'

'I don't know,' she said. She had already voiced her darkest fear. And it didn't lose any of its power just because her objective brain knew it was unlikely. 'Do you think I'm completely irrational?'

Fraser shook his head and reached for her

hand. 'I think you love your sister and you've spent your whole life putting her first. But now she's grown up I think she wants to take care of herself.'

'I don't know if I can just...stop caring. Stop being afraid.'

He squeezed her fingers, caught her eye and smiled. 'Well, then, it's a good job you don't have to do it by yourself. We'll work it out between us. *All* of us. In our own time.'

Elspeth brushed away a tear with the back of her hand.

'I asked you earlier what you want. You never gave me an answer,' he reminded her.

She reached up on her tiptoes, aware of her bump between them as she wrapped her arms around his neck and pulled him down to her, finally breaching those millimetres between their lips that had been driving her insane, making it impossible for her to think straight.

He let her come to him, true to his word, letting her lead, not demanding more from her than she was giving. But there was a time and a place for being restrained, and right now she wanted the Fraser who had pinned her wrists and made her moan the night they had met. She pressed harder against him, letting her fingers tighten slightly in his hair.

'God, Fraser,' she said between kisses. 'Of course I want *you*. You know I do.'

Another kiss and her hand was tangling in his hair. The other hand was exploring his shoulders. His back. Pulling at his shirt and diving for the skin beneath.

'I don't know how this is going to work…' she said suddenly, feeling a shot of reality start a slow puncture in their bubble.

'Stop thinking,' Fraser demanded, angling his head to deepen their kiss.

The heat of his tongue in her mouth sent a shot of desire straight through her belly, and the feel of his hands exploring her waist, her breasts, her bottom, had her wishing she had somewhere to take him that didn't share a flimsy plasterboard wall with her mother or her sister.

That thought acted like a pitcher of iced water to the back of the neck and she pushed Fraser away slightly, gasping for breath as she tried to collect her thoughts.

'Rethinking the whole living together thing?' Fraser asked with a wry smile, equally breathless, reading her thoughts faster than she could form them.

'For tonight. Definitely. After that…'

'After that we'll figure it out. I can't promise you easy answers, Elspeth. But I promise you that I'll be here. I promise you that we will do this together. We'll find something that works for all of us.'

She rested her head against his chest and smiled as his hands came round to her belly, rubbing, encouraging, until he was rewarded with a kick.

Fraser cupped her chin, tipped her face up to his for a light kiss on the lips.

'I love you,' Fraser said, his gaze locked on hers. 'And I want you every day. I don't care that this is the scariest thing I've ever done—I'm not going to run from it. I believe we can do this. I believe *you* can do this. And any time you doubt that, doubt us, I'm going to be here to remind you that we love each other enough to make this work.'

She didn't doubt him for a second—she

couldn't when the truth of his words was written in every smiling line around his eyes. She stood with that feeling for a moment—the knowledge that they were in this together, the warm satisfaction of knowing that someone loved her as passionately as she knew Fraser did. That everything they would face, they would face together. Her heart was now part of something bigger than her. Something bigger than either of them.

She let the words settle into the quiet of the kitchen.

'I love you too,' she said at last. 'And I'm not just saying that because you did. I'm saying it because I can't live without you, Fraser. I want you in my life for ever. I want us to belong to each other for ever.'

Fraser pressed his lips against hers again and the kiss was sweet this time, rather than holding the fire they had shared before. Sealing the promises they had just made to each other. When he pulled away he was smiling, but she sensed a nervous anticipation in him as he reached for where he had left his jacket on the counter and pulled out a small leather box.

'Well, then, I'd better give you this,' Fraser said, lifting the lid to reveal a delicate platinum band with a channel of diamonds set smoothly into the metal.

Elspeth took the box from him, her mouth open in surprise as she looked from the ring up to Fraser's face.

'I was going to break up with you,' she said, a ghost of a smile on her lips.

'I know. And if you'd told me that you didn't love me and you didn't want to be with me you'd have never known that this existed.'

'But you thought you might be able to talk me round?'

'I hoped,' he said, pulling her tight against him. 'I hoped like I swear I have never hoped before that I wouldn't have to. That I was right to trust in what I feel. That I was right to think that you love me, and that what we share will be strong enough to survive this.'

'You have a lot of faith in me. In us.'

He nodded. 'I have faith in you. And I have faith that I know how to make you happy.'

'You know that I come as a package deal? Do you really want to move in here?'

He shrugged. 'I would do it in a heartbeat if you asked. *Are* you asking?'

'Are *you* asking?' Elspeth said, her face breaking out into a grin. 'Diamond rings usually come with a question.'

He laughed, tucking a lock of hair behind her ear and taking the ring back from her.

'You're right. I'm doing this all wrong.'

Keeping hold of her hand, he dropped to one knee in front of her.

'Elspeth, I have wanted you every day for the last six months, and I will love you every day for the rest of my life. Will you please put me out of my misery and agree to be my wife?'

She looked down into the face of the man she loved and saw all the possibilities for their future in his hopeful gaze. 'I will, Fraser. I love you and I'll be your wife tomorrow if I can.'

She pulled him up by the hands until he was standing in front of her, then wound her arms round his neck and pulled him in close.

Fraser laughed, the deep, rich timbre of his mirth muffled by her hair. 'I'm more than tempted to take you up on that, but I trust that you're not going to change your mind. Anyway, now this wee bairn is so close…' he smoothed a gentle hand around her bump '… I'd quite like to share the day with him, or her. What do you think?'

'I think that sounds perfect,' Elspeth replied, her face buried in his neck. 'I think that sounds like everything I've ever wanted.'

EPILOGUE

As Elspeth rapped her knuckles on the black front door, the sunlight caught the pretty row of diamonds on the third finger of her left hand and she smiled, wondering if she would ever get used to seeing them there. If she would ever glance at them and not be reminded of that evening in her mum's kitchen, when she had realised that despite all her best efforts to sabotage things Fraser loved her, and he wasn't going to let her go. That, despite years of telling herself that she couldn't have everything that she wanted, she was getting all that and more.

She dropped her hand back to her side and Fraser's fingers curled through hers with an intimacy that was nowhere close to losing its thrill.

The door opened in front of them and Sarah

was waiting for them in the hallway, beaming with happiness and pride. 'Come in!' she said. 'Where is she? Where's my niece?'

Elspeth glanced across at the car seat Fraser was carrying beside him and was almost overwhelmed by tears at the sight of her baby daughter, tucked up in a blanket and snoring gently.

'She's so beautiful,' Sarah said, mirroring Elspeth's smile, causing more tears to well up. 'Come through to the living room—I'm desperate to cuddle her.'

'I'm to warn you that there are severe penalties for waking a sleeping baby,' Fraser said, in a voice of mock seriousness.

'That's an auntie's prerogative, surely?' Sarah fired back, pulling her chair up beside the sofa where Fraser had left the car seat in order to get a better look at the baby. 'Does she have a name yet?'

Elspeth glanced at Fraser. 'We're thinking maybe… Isabel. But we haven't set our minds yet.'

'Plenty of time to get to know her,' Fraser

said, smiling at Elspeth and then beaming at his daughter.

It was something else she would never tire of, she realised, that expression. The pure joy and pride and love when he looked at their baby. It was everything she had dreamed of since she had found out that she was pregnant. Before she had even thought to dream of him for herself.

The baby snuffled, grunted and pursed her lips, and Fraser, Elspeth and Sarah all laughed quietly.

'I guess that's my cue to get comfy on the sofa,' Elspeth said, scooping the baby up and latching her on for a feed. 'You said on the phone you needed Fraser to do you a favour? You should get him while you can. We're thinking of going up to Ballanross for a few weeks, making the most of my maternity leave and spending some time there.'

'I think I'm going to like having a brother-in-law,' Sarah said. 'He volunteers for DIY and he brings a castle into the family. I'll like him even better when I get to see Ballanross for myself. How's the building work going?'

'Slowly,' Fraser said, his face serious for a moment. 'But we're doing it right. We're re-building the estate from top to bottom, and eventually we'll be self-sufficient again. By the time this wee one is old enough to remember,' he said, and smiled across at the baby, 'it'll be just how I knew it.'

Elspeth squeezed his hand, watching the interaction between her fiancée and her sister, seeing how they were supporting each other and feeling a warm glow of happiness.

Fraser had played an invaluable part in getting Sarah's apartment ready. It had taken a lot of planning, and a leap of faith and confidence, but Sarah had been determined to move into a flat on her own, and Elspeth had finally seen that it was up to her to support her sister's dreams—not get in the way. And now she was here, and she could see the pride on Sarah's face as she showed them round her new flat, showed them the changes that had been made since she had first moved in a couple of weeks ago.

Which was why Elspeth was curious about what Sarah needed Fraser for. They'd had a team of builders in here to make sure the flat was perfectly adapted for Sarah and her carers. She'd thought it had all been taken care of already. But if her sister needed a favour, and Fraser was happy to help out, then who was she to interfere?

She pulled a cushion from the other end of the sofa and tucked it under her arm, looking down and watching the baby's perfect round cheeks wobble as she fed.

Fraser returned, carrying a very large box and with a smile on his face. Sarah was just behind him.

She pointed at the large blank space above the TV. 'Right, you and I are going to direct, Elspeth, and Fraser is going to do the heavy lifting.'

'Okay…' Elspeth said, as if she had an idea what her sister was talking about.

She'd found, over the years, that it was often just easier to go along with Sarah when she had one of her grand plans. Now she'd realised that her sister was perfectly capable of making her own decisions about where to live, she couldn't really dispute what she planned to do now she was all moved in.

'Where do you think we should hang this one?'

From the box Fraser pulled out a framed photo of Elspeth, Sarah and their mum, and held it against the wall.

Elspeth beamed—she'd had no idea that Sarah had been planning this. 'It's lovely,' she said with a broad grin. 'Centre of the fireplace, surely? Pride of place.'

Sarah agreed, so Fraser propped the frame against the wall and went back to the box.

He pulled out another picture—this one of Elspeth and Sarah, wrapped in a tight hug. Elspeth felt another wave of tears well up and knew she was fighting a losing battle. She smiled at her sister, who was watching her indulgently.

'And the last one?' Sarah said, gesturing for Fraser to get on with it, clearly still excited.

Fraser pulled out the final picture, and Elspeth gasped. It was her and Fraser and the baby, just hours after she had been born, still shell-shocked and dazed in the hospital.

'I want you all right here on my wall,' Sarah said. 'Just because I wanted to move out it doesn't mean I'm not going to miss you.'

Elspeth passed the now-sleeping baby to Fraser and squeezed her sister into a hug. 'I miss you too. But I'm so proud of you,' she added. 'I've always known that you could do this. I'm so sorry that I wasn't brave enough to let you do it sooner.'

'You got there in the end,' Sarah said with a smile. 'And you brought these two along with you, so I guess it was worth it.'

Elspeth glanced from Sarah to Fraser and then down to the baby, who was still fast asleep in his arms, and couldn't imagine any greater pleasure than this. Knowing that the people she loved most in the world were happy, safe, secure. Grateful and full of wonder that they had all been courageous enough to trust that their love for one another would be enough to make this a reality…to make them a family.

* * * * *